新·编·大·学·英·语·教·学·配·套·丛·书

U0141000

大学英语

新题型 ④ 级

分级教学同步训练

College English Practice Tests | Band **4**

总 主 编　李予军
本册主编　赵　军
副 主 编　韩鹤勤
编　　者　杜　曼
　　　　　张　宁

国防工业出版社
National Defense Industry Press

内容简介

本书是《新编大学英语教学配套丛书》的第 4 册,内容达到大学英语四级水平要求;在题型编排设计上既考虑学生学习现状,又兼顾大学英语四级考试的试题形式,使学生能把学习内容和测试形式结合起来,有针对性地达到训练的目的。全书包括训练试题10 套,内容涵盖写作、听力理解和听力填空、阅读词汇理解、篇章阅读、阅读简答、词汇和翻译等。书后附有参考答案和听力部分的录音原文。

本书可供大学基础阶段二年级的学生或相当于四级水平的英语学习爱好者使用。

图书在版编目(CIP)数据

大学英语分级教学同步训练新题型 4 级/赵军
主编.—北京:国防工业出版社,2008.9
(新编大学英语教学配套丛书)
ISBN 978-7-118-05933-5

Ⅰ.大... Ⅱ.赵... Ⅲ.英语 – 高等学校 – 习题
Ⅳ.H319.6

中国版本图书馆 CIP 数据核字(2008)第 135129 号

※

*国防工业出版社*出版发行
(北京市海淀区紫竹院南路 23 号 邮政编码 100044)
天利华印刷装订有限公司印刷
新华书店经售

*

开本 787×1092 1/16 印张 13¼ 字数 260 千字
2008 年 9 月第 1 版第 1 次印刷 印数 1—5000 册 定价 25.00 元(含光盘)

(本书如有印装错误,我社负责调换)

国防书店:(010)68428422   发行邮购:(010)68414474
发行传真:(010)68411535   发行业务:(010)68472764

前　言

大学英语教学改革是教育部"高等学校教学改革与教学质量工程"的重要组成部分。《新编大学英语教学配套丛书》正是根据教育部颁发的《大学英语课程教学要求》(以下简称《课程要求》)和《大学英语四、六级考试改革方案(试行)》的精神,结合高校一线教师在大学英语一级至四级的教学和研究中所积累的经验和资料,针对学生在学习、考试中反映出来的问题编写而成的,是探索大学英语教学改革,改进教学模式和教学方法,提高教学效果的一次新尝试。

大学英语的教学目的是培养学生的英语综合应用能力。《课程要求》提出各校应根据实际情况制定科学、系统、个性化的大学英语教学大纲,指导本校的大学英语教学。大学阶段英语教学的一般要求是高等学校非英语专业本科毕业生应达到的基本要求。较高要求或更高要求是为有条件的学校根据自己的办学定位、类型和人才培养目标所选择的标准而推荐的。各高等学校应根据本校实际情况确定教学目标并创造条件,使那些英语起点水平较高、学有余力的学生能够达到较高要求或更高要求。这是本丛书编写的理论依据。

近年来,一大批专科院校纷纷"升本"。这些院校基本都定位于"应用型"大学,即把培养应用型人才作为自己的培养目标;同时,这些院校还有一个共同的特点,就是生源基本来自"三本"学生。这两个实际情况就决定了这些院校的大学英语教学必须走自己的特色之路,既要努力达到一般要求的规定,又要保证满足一些水平较好的学生的求知欲望。这是本丛书编写的现实依据。

《课程要求》指出,教学评估是大学英语课程教学的一个重要环节。全面、客观、科学、准确的评估体系对于实现教学目标至关重要。过去过于关注期中和期末考试,并一度出现"以考代学,以考代教"的现象,导致教学效果不佳,甚至停滞不前。形成性评估是教学过程中进行的过程性和发展性评估,即根据教学目标采用多种评估手段和形式,跟踪教学过程,反馈教学信息,促进学生全面发展。这是本丛书编写的基本指导思想。

本丛书主要是配合大学英语教学之用,分为新题型 1 级、2 级、3 级、4 级和 4 级冲刺,共 5 册,分别供大学基础阶段二学年 4 个学期使用,一学期一级,与教材和教学同步配套使用。每册由 3 个部分组成:(1)完整的标准模拟试题 10 套;(2)参考答案和听力原文;(3)配套光盘一张。

本丛书有以下几个主要特点:

1. 严格按照《课程要求》规定和《大学英语四、六级考试改革方案(试行)》的要求,力求体现科学性、实用性和针对性,总结实际教学过程中的经验,结合学生学习的现状,按照标准化的四级考试新题型编写而成,力争突出教材中的重点和难点,旨在通过这些综合内容测试训练,考察学生在综合知识和能力上的掌握程度,并以此作为形成性评估的重要依据和手段。

2. 严格按照《课程要求》精神和规定,突出分级分层教学理念。丛书各分册的内容都分别精选或参考各高校目前的主打教材,紧扣教学内容和教学进度,力求把每册各单元的课程目标和课文重点、难点融入综合测试当中,特别是学生感到难以突破的词汇、完型、翻译和写作;注重学生综合能力和应用能力的培养,既能促进学生有效地掌握语言相关知识和基本技能,又能培养学生自觉的学习意识,开发自主性学习方法。

3. 本丛书各分册试题都是经过精心挑选配套完成的,试题之间、每册之间都有侧重并在难易程度上有区别,特别是在听力、写作题目和要求上更是如此。这既有助于学生在学习过程中注意由易到难的循序过程,也便于教师在教学中不断掌握学生的学习动态,及时调整教学进度和内容。

4. 本丛书既可以作为大学英语教学同步配套教材,也可以用于学生自学自测;既可以整套使用,也可以按需分开使用,以适用于不同阶段不同程度的学生,真正体现出分层、分级、同步和实用,达到训练的目的。另外,本丛书也可供大学基础阶段准备参加各级各类英语考试的学生使用。

参加本丛书编写的人员都是来自首都高校教学第一线的骨干教师,年富力强,具有丰富的教学经验,在编写丛书的同时,也融入了他们自己的教学理念。

在编写过程中,我们参考了部分教科书、参考书和网站的内容,在此特向有关作者、出版单位和网站表示诚挚的谢意。

由于时间仓促,书中难免会有不足之处,恳请广大读者提出宝贵意见和建议。本丛书在编写过程中得到有关方面的大力支持,在此表示衷心的感谢。

编 者

Contents

Model Test 1

Part One Writing

Directions: *For this part, you are allowed thirty minutes to write a composition on the topic* **What Would Happen If There Were No Power** *in three paragraphs. You are given the first sentence or part of the first sentence of each paragraph. Your part of the composition should be no less than 120 words, not including the words given.*

What Would Happen If There Were No Power

1. Ever since early last century, electricity has become an essential part of our modern life.

2. If there were no electric power,_____.

3. Therefore,_____.

Part Two Listening Comprehension

Section A

Directions: *In this section you will hear 10 short conversations. At the end of each conversation, a question will be asked about what was said, both the conversation and the question will be spoken only once. After each question there will be a pause. During the pause, you must read the four choices marked A, B, C and D, and decide which is the best answer. Then mark the corresponding letter on the Answer sheet with a single line through the center.*

1. A. The flight has been cancelled because of bad weather.
   B. The plane will arrive at 9:50.
   C. The plane will arrive after 9:50.
   D. The plane will be late because of a heavy storm.

2. A. She enjoys seeing films very much.

   B. She's taking an exam on Sunday.

   C. She does not enjoy seeing films very much.

   D. She has to review her lessons at weekends.

3. A. He is attending his sick mother at home.

   B. He is on a European tour with his mother.

   C. He is at home on sick leave.

   D. He is in Europe to see his mother.

4. A. 450 million.

   B. 400 million.

   C. 550 million.

   D. 470 million.

5. A. In a wheat field.

   B. At a railway station.

   C. On a farm.

   D. On a train.

6. A. She is sure who is going to win.

   B. Now it's a good time to start the game.

   C. The game has been going on for a long time.

   D. The same team always wins.

7. A. He enjoys writing home every week.

   B. He does not write home once a week now.

   C. He never fails to write a weekly letter home.

   D. He has been asked to write home every week.

8. A. She's already visited the museum.

   B. Mary might be leaving earlier than she is.

   C. Mary will take him to the school.

   D. The man could probably go with Mary.

9. A. Jim is at a meeting now.

   B. Jim's roommate is out.

   C. Jim had moved to another room

   D. Jim is with his girlfriend now.

10. A. Go and listen to music.

B. Try to get some tickets.

C. Go and buy a new dress.

D. Make preparation for class presentation.

Section B

Directions: *In this section, you will hear three short passages. At the end of each passage, you will hear some questions. Both the passage and the questions will be spoken only once. After you hear a question, you must choose the best answer from the four choices marked A, B, C and D, and decide which is the best answer. Then mark the corresponding letter on the Answer Sheet with a single line through the center.*

Passage 1

Questions 11 to 13 are based on the passage you have just heard.

11. A. Watching traditional plays.

    B. Visiting the magnificent libraries.

    C. Boating on the river.

    D. Cycling in narrow streets.

12. A. There are many visitors there.

    B. There are many students there.

    C. There are many old streets there.

    D. There are many bicycles there.

13. A. He thinks the city is too crowded.

    B. He likes the place very much.

    C. He thinks the streets are too narrow.

    D. He admires the comfortable life of the students there.

Passage 2

Questions 14 to 16 are based on the passage you have just heard.

14. A. Other employees would not want to work under him.

    B. Other employees were better qualified.

    C. Other employees wanted the job themselves.

    D. Other employees had carried no responsibility.

15. A. He is a black man.

  B. He was too qualified.

  C. The jobs were not well paid.

  D. They carried no responsibility.

16. A. The decision made him feel ill.

  B. The decision disappointed him.

  C. The decision made him feel angry.

  D. The decision came as a shock to him.

Passage 3

Question 17 to 20 are based on the passage you have just heard.

17. A. Two-year-old.

  B. Twenty-year-old.

  C. Twelve-year-old.

  D. Not know.

18. A. A boy shouted for help while swimming.

  B. A young man dived into the river and rescued him.

  C. A small crowd collected along the bank.

  D. All of the above.

19. A. He thanked the young man and put down his name.

  B. He thanked the young man and ran away.

  C. He said nothing and went on swimming.

  D. He said he would thank the young man later.

20. A. The boy was good at swimming.

  B. The young man was good at swimming.

  C. The boy didn't give his name.

  D. The young man didn't give his name.

Section C

Directions: *In this section, you will hear a passage of about 150 words three times. The passage is printed on your Answer Sheet with about 15 words missing. First you will hear the whole passage from the beginning to the end just to get a general idea of it. Then, in the second reading, you will hear a sig-*

nal indicating the beginning of a pause after each sentence, sometimes two sentences or just part of a sentence. During the pause, you must write down the missing words you have just heard in the corresponding space on the Answer Sheet. There is also a different signal indicating the end of the pause. When you hear this signal, you must get ready for what comes next from the recording. You can check what you have written when the passage is read to you once again without the pauses.

A passage with 15 missing words

Martin Luther King, Jr. was born in Atlanta, Georgia, on ___(21)___ 15, 1929. He was a black ___(22)___, who devoted himself ___(23)___ to the struggle for ___(24)___ rights for the black people and an end to segregation in the South of the United States. In ___(25)___, he organized a black boycott of the city buses in Montgomery, Alabama. The black people there had ___(26)___ that they would no longer ___(27)___ in segregated buses. Led by King, they ___(28)___ to the courts for support of their ___(29)___ The boycott against segregation lasted 381 days, and ended in ___(30)___ the next year.

In the spring of 1963, he began to organize a ___(31)___ to Washington to persuade the U. S. government to ___(32)___ a mass Civil Rights Movement for black people. ___(33)___. From all over the country, citizens came to "march on Washington" in support of civil rights legislation. It was then that King delivered the most impressive speech of his career. ___(34)___.

In 1964, at the age of only 35, he was awarded the Nobel Peace Prize. ___(35)___.

Part Three   Reading Comprehension

Directions: *In this section, there is a passage with 10 blanks. You are required to select one word for each blank from a list of choices given in a word bank following the passage. Read the passage through carefully before making your choices. Each choice in the bank is identified by a letter. Please mark the corresponding letter for each item on Answer Sheet with a single line through the center.* **You may not use any of words in the bank more than once.**

A passage with 10 blanks

When the earth was born there was no ocean. The gradually cooling earth was enveloped in heavy layers of cloud, which ___(36)___ much of the water of new planet. For a long time its surface was so hot that no moisture could fall without ___(37)___ Being reconverted to steam. This dense, perpetually renewed cloud covering much have been so ___(38)___ that no rays of sunlight could penetrate it. And so the rough ___(39)___ of the continents and the empty ocean basins(盆地) were sculptured out of the surface of the earth in ___(40)___ .

As soon as the earth's crust cooled enough, the rains begin to fall. They fell ___(41)___ day and night, days passing into months, into years, into centuries. They ___(42)___ into the waiting ocean basins, or, falling upon the continental masses, drained away to become sea.

That primeval(原始的) ocean must have been only faintly ___(43)___ But from the moment the rains began to fall, the lands began to be ___(44)___ away and carried to the sea. It is an endless, inexorable(不可动摇的) ___(45)___ that has never stopped—the dissolving of the rocks, the leaching out of their contained minerals, the carrying of the rock fragments and dissolved minerals to the ocean. And over the long periods of time, the sea has grown ever more bitter with the salt of the continents.

A. thick	E. brightness	I. salty	M. worn
B. darkness	F. procedure	J. immediately	N. poured
C. composed	G. outlines	K. process	O. abundant
D. continuously	H. contained	L. successively	

Section B

Directions: *There are 2 passages in this section. Each passage is followed by some questions or unfinished statements. For each of them there are four choices marked A, B, C and D. You should decide on the best choice and mark the corresponding letter on Answer Sheet with a single line through the center.*

Passage 1

Questions 46 to 50 are based on the following passage.

The World Health Organization says as many as 10 million persons worldwide may have the virus (病毒) that causes AIDS. Experts believe about 350 thousand persons have the disease. And one million more may get it in the next five years. In the United States, about 50,000 persons have died with AIDS. The country's top medical official says more than

90 percent of all Americans who had the AIDS virus five years ago are dead.

There is no cure for AIDS and no vaccine(疫苗)medicine to prevent it. However, researchers know much more about AIDS than they did just a few years ago. We now know that AIDS is caused by a virus. The virus invades healthy cells including white blood cells that are part of our defense system against disease. It takes control of the healthy cell's genetic(遗传的) material and forces the cell to make a copy of the virus. The cell then dies. And the viral particles move on to invade and kill more healthy cells. The AIDS virus is carried in a person's body fluids. The virus can be passed sexually or by sharing instruments used to take intravenous(静脉内的)drugs. It also can be passed in blood products or from a pregnant woman with AIDS to her developing baby.

Many stories about the spread of AIDS are false. You cannot get AIDS by working or attending school with someone who has the disease. You can not get it by touching, drinking glasses or other objects used by such persons. Experts say no one has gotten AIDS by living with, caring for or touching an AIDS patient.

There are several warning signs of an AIDS infection. They include always feeling tired, unexplained weight loss and uncontrolled expulsion of body wastes(大小便失禁). Other warnings are the appearance of white areas on the mouth, dark red areas of skin that do not disappear and a higher than normal body temperature.

46. Which of the following statements is NOT mentioned in the passage?

   A. As many as 350 thousand persons have AIDS.

   B. The AIDS virus is carried in a person's body fluids.

   C. There's no vaccine medicine to prevent AIDS.

   D. The AIDS virus is not spread by mosquitoes.

47. Concerning the ways the AIDS virus can be passed, which of the following statements is wrong?

   A. An AIDS mother can pass on the virus to her unborn child.

   B. The AIDS virus can be passed on through infected blood.

   C. The AIDS virus can be passed on by shaking hands and sharing belongings.

   D. The AIDS virus is passed sexually.

48. The expression "a pregnant woman"(Para. 2) means _____.

   A. a woman who has an unborn child in the body

   B. a woman who is taking drug

C. a woman who has the AIDS virus

D. an unmarried mother

49. The fourth paragraph is mainly about _____.

    A. the results of an AIDS infection

    B. the possible symptoms of an AIDS infection

    C. how the AIDS virus is spread

    D. the diseases AIDS patients easily have

50. When the AIDS virus attacks our defense system, _____.

    A. it starts to destroy our white blood cells

    B. we begin to feel tired

    C. it means we will die very soon

    D. our white blood cells can control it

Passage 2

Questions 51 to 55 are based on the following passage.

As soon as it was revealed that a reporter for Progressive magazine had discovered how to make a hydrogen bomb, a group of firearm (火器) fans formed the National Hydrogen Bomb Association, and they are now lobbying against any legislation to stop Americans from owning one.

"The Constitution," said the association's spokesman, "gives everyone the right to own arms. It doesn't spell out what kind of arms. But since anyone can now make a hydrogen bomb, the public should be able to buy it to protect themselves."

"Don't you think it's dangerous to have one in the house, particularly where there are children around?"

"The National Hydrogen Bomb Association hopes to educate people in the safe handling of this type of weapon. We are instructing owners to keep the bomb in a locked cabinet and the fuse (导火索) separately in a drawer."

"Some people consider the hydrogen bomb a very fatal weapon which could kill somebody."

The spokesman said, "Hydrogen bombs don't kill people — people kill people. The bomb is for self-protection and it also has a deterrent effect. If somebody knows you have a nuclear weapon in your house, they're going to think twice about breaking in".

"But those who want to ban the bomb for American citizens claim that if you have one locked in the cabinet, with the fuse in a drawer, you would never be able to assemble it in time to stop an intruder (侵入者)".

"Another argument against allowing people to own a bomb is that at the moment it is very expensive to build one. So what your association is backing is a program which would allow the middle and upper classes to acquire a bomb while poor people will be left defenseless with just handguns."

51. According to the passage, some people started a national association so as to _____ .

   A. instruct people how to keep the bomb safe at home

   B. coordinate the mass production of the destructive weapon

   C. promote the large-scale sale of this newly invented weapon

   D. Block any legislation to ban the private possession of the bomb

52. Some people oppose the ownership of H-bombs by individuals on the grounds that

   _____ .

   A. they may fall into the hands of criminals

   B. people's lives will be threatened by the weapon

   C. most people don't know how to handle the weapon

   D. the size of the bomb makes it difficult to keep in a drawer

53. By saying that the bomb also has a deterrent effect the spokesman means that it

   _____ .

   A. can kill those entering others' houses by force

   B. will threaten the safety of the owners as well

   C. will frighten away any possible intruders

   D. can show the special status of its owners

54. According to the passage, opponents of the private ownership of H-bombs are very much worried that _____ .

   A. the cost of the weapon will put citizens on an unequal basis

   B. the wide use of the weapon will push up living expenses tremendously

   C. poorly-educated Americans will find it difficult to make use of the weapon

   D. the influence of the association is too powerful for the less privileged to overcome

55. From the tone of the passage we know that the author is _____ .

   A. not serious about the private ownership of H-bombs

   B. concerned about the spread of nuclear weapons

C. doubtful about the necessity of keeping H-bombs at home for safety

D. unhappy with those who vote against the ownership of H-bombs

Part Four   Vocabulary

Directions: *Fou this part you are required to choose the best answer from A, B, C and D to complete the following sentences.*

56. You are very _____ to take the trouble to help me. I can not thank you enough.

    A. whisper   B. vital   C. thoughtful   D. considerable

57. What's your favorite kind of music? Do you like _____ music?

    A. domestic   B. classical   C. existence   D. feature

58. This nation is noted for its economic _____.

    A. uniform   B. stability   C. gulf   D. democratic

59. He wants to _____ his appointment from Monday to Wednesday.

    A. transfer   B. decay   C. advance   D. postpone

60. This is what I could do. There is no other _____ for me.

    A. sleeve   B. residence   C. burden   D. alternative

61. Our teacher always sees the _____ side of everything.

    A. spot   B. negative   C. efficient   D. robot

62. If you want to make a call, first, pick up the _____, then deposit a coin in the slot.

    A. receiver   B. speaker   C. microphone   D. hook

63. The service in this restaurant is not good Even the _____ is very dirty.

    A. milk   B. salad   C. soup   D. menu

64. I am _____ enough to make up my own mind. You do not need to teach me.

    A. young   B. mature   C. numerical   D. guarantee

65. I'm _____ you've made the right choice.

    A. bond   B. confident   C. double   D. gravity

66. Kuwait is famous for its _____ resources.

    A. petroleum   B. jar   C. fame   D. jaw

67. The doctor gave me a chest X-ray and _____ some medicine for me.

    A. prescribed   B. floated   C. drugged   D. drifted

68. Nobody believes he made such a foolish mistake. People say he is very _____.

    A. accurate   B. actual   C. experience   D. career

10

69. The _____ region is centered largely in the north of the country.

    A. petrol   B. mineral   C. telescope   D. wire

70. As soon as I complete my training here, I am going to be a _____ expert.

    A. sphere   B. missile   C. rod   D. volume

71. I was crossing the street and was almost hit by an _____ .

    A. ambulance   B. amateur   C. echo   D. editor

72. How much do you know about the works of great _____ figures?

    A. literary   B. humour   C. grammatical   D. circular

73. The next time I buy a typewriter, I'm going to buy a _____ model.

    A. sulphur   B. portable   C. suspending   D. tender

74. Your _____ for this paper is too long to be accepted.

    A. entrance   B. guidance   C. abstract   D. represent

75. Water is as _____ to fish as air is to man.

    A. obvious   B. basin   C. indispensable   D. constant

Part Five   Short Answer Questions

Directions: *In this part there is a short passage with five questions or incomplete statements. Read the passage carefully. Then answer the questions or complete the statement in the fewest possible words.*

Questions 76 to 80 are based on the passage.

A man's skin is thicker than a woman's and not nearly as soft. The thickness prevents the sun's radiation from getting through, which is why men wrinkle less than women do.

Women have a thin layer of fat just under the skin and there is a plus(有利因素) to this greater fat reserve. It acts as an invisible fur coat to keep a woman warmer in the winter.

Women also stay cooler in summer. The fat layer helps insulate them against heat.

Men's fat is distributed differently. And they do not have that layer of it underneath their skin. In fact, they have considerably less fat than women and more lean mass. Forty-one percent of a man's body is muscle compared to thirty-five percent for women, which means men have more muscle power. When it comes to strength, almost 90 percent of a man's weight is stronger compared to about 50 percent of a woman' weight.

The higher proportion of muscle to fat makes it easier for men to lose weight. Muscle burns up five more calories a pound than fat does just to maintain itself. So when a man goes on a diet, the pounds roll off much faster.

For all men's muscularity they do not have the energy reserves as women do. They have more start-up energy, but the fat tucked away in women's nooks and crannies(隐匿处)provides a rich energy reserve that men lack.

Cardiologists(心脏病专家)at the University of Alabama who tested healthy women on treadmills(单调而又劳累的活)discovered that over years the female capacity for exercise far exceeds the male capacity. A woman of sixty who is in good health can exercise up to 90 percent of what she could do when she was twenty. A man of sixty has only 60 percent left of his capacity as a twenty-year-old.

76. The title of the passage can be _____ .

77. What makes men wrinkle less than women? _____ .

78. The thin layer of fat under women's skin keeps _____ in summer.

79. The proportion of muscle to fat explains why it is _____ for women to lose weight compared with men.

80. It is implied that the process of aging is _____ in a healthy woman.

Part Six   Translation

Directions: *Finish the sentences on Answer Sheet by translating into English*.

81. (他花了大量的时间准备数学考试)_____ . Hence he was somewhat disappointed to learn that he got only a B.

82. Next Tuesday is the deadline for handing in the term papers, _____ (但是大多数学生到目前为止还没有任何进展).

83. I'd rather you _____ (礼貌地对她讲话).

84. People today are more mobile than ever before; perhaps _____ (这就是为什么手机已变得很普通的原因).

85. _____ (令我们宽慰的是),our performance was fully appreciated by the audience, mostly college students.

Answer Sheet

Part One   Writing

What Would Happen If There Were No Power

_____

_____

_____

_____

_____

_____

_____

_____

_____

_____

_____

_____

_____

_____

_____

_____

_____

_____

_____

_____

Part Two　Listening Comprehension

Section A

1. [A][B][C][D]　2. [A][B][C][D]　3. [A][B][C][D]　4. [A][B][C][D]
5. [A][B][C][D]　6. [A][B][C][D]　7. [A][B][C][D]　8. [A][B][C][D]
9. [A][B][C][D]　10. [A][B][C][D]

Section B

11. [A][B][C][D] 12. [A][B][C][D]　13. [A][B][C][D]　14. [A][B][C][D]
15. [A][B][C][D] 16. [A][B][C][D]　17. [A][B][C][D]　18. [A][B][C][D]
19. [A][B][C][D] 20. [A][B][C][D]

Section C

21. _____　22. _____　23. _____　24. _____　25. _____
26. _____　27. _____　28. _____　29. _____　30. _____
31. _____　32. _____

33. _____

34. _____

35. _____

Part Three　Reading Comprehension

Section A   Section B

36. [A][B][C][D][E][F][G][H][I][J][K][L][M][N][O]　46. [A][B][C][D]
37. [A][B][C][D][E][F][G][H][I][J][K][L][M][N][O]　47. [A][B][C][D]
38. [A][B][C][D][E][F][G][H][I][J][K][L][M][N][O]　48. [A][B][C][D]
39. [A][B][C][D][E][F][G][H][I][J][K][L][M][N][O]　49. [A][B][C][D]
40. [A][B][C][D][E][F][G][H][I][J][K][L][M][N][O]　50. [A][B][C][D]
41. [A][B][C][D][E][F][G][H][I][J][K][L][M][N][O]　51. [A][B][C][D]
42. [A][B][C][D][E][F][G][H][I][J][K][L][M][N][O]　52. [A][B][C][D]
43. [A][B][C][D][E][F][G][H][I][J][K][L][M][N][O]　53. [A][B][C][D]
44. [A][B][C][D][E][F][G][H][I][J][K][L][M][N][O]　54. [A][B][C][D]
45. [A][B][C][D][E][F][G][H][I][J][K][L][M][N][O]　55. [A][B][C][D]

Part Four   Vocabulary

56. [A][B][C][D] 57. [A][B][C][D] 58. [A][B][C][D] 59. [A][B][C][D]
60. [A][B][C][D] 61. [A][B][C][D] 62. [A][B][C][D] 63. [A][B][C][D]
64. [A][B][C][D] 65. [A][B][C][D] 66. [A][B][C][D] 67. [A][B][C][D]
68. [A][B][C][D] 69. [A][B][C][D] 70. [A][B][C][D] 71. [A][B][C][D]
72. [A][B][C][D] 73. [A][B][C][D] 74. [A][B][C][D] 75. [A][B][C][D]

Part Five   Short Answer Questions

76. The title of the passage can be _____.

77. What makes men wrinkle less than women? _____.

78. The thin layer of fat under women's skin keep _____. in summer.

79. The proportion of muscle to fat explains why it is _____ for women to lose weight compared with men.

80. It is implied that the process of aging is _____ in a healthy woman.

Part Six   Translation

81. _____

82. _____

83. _____

84. _____

85. _____

Model Test 2

Part One   Writing

Directions: *For this part, you are allowed thirty minutes to write a letter. Suppose you are Liu Ying. Write a letter to Nancy, a schoolmate of yours who is going to visit you during the week-long holiday. You should write at least 100 words according to the suggestions given below in Chinese.*

1. 表示欢迎；
2. 提出对度假安排的建议；
3. 提醒应注意的事项。

A letter to a Schoolmate

Part Two   Listening Comprehension

Section A

Directions: *In this section you will hear 10 short conversations. At the end of each conversation, a question will be asked about what was said, both the conversation and the question will be spoken only once. After each question there will be a pause. During the pause, you must read the four choices marked A, B, C and D, and decide which is the best answer. Then mark the corresponding letter on the Answer sheet with a single line through the center.*

1. A. He wants to make an appointment with Dr Li.
   B. He wants to make sure that Dr. Li will see him.
   C. He wants to change the time of the appointment.
   D. He wants the woman to meet him at two o'clock.
2. A. Librarian and student.

16

B. Operator and caller.

C. Boss and secretary.

D. Customer and repairman.

3. A. Looking for a timetable.

B. Reserving a table.

C. Buying some furniture.

D. Window shopping.

4. A. The woman should buy some new clothes.

B. The woman should buy some clothes of a larger size.

C. The woman should eat less.

D. The woman should do more exercises.

5. A. Linda should spend more time studying.

B. Linda really needs a full-time job.

C. Linda should do more housework at home.

D. Linda shouldn't study too hard.

6. A. 7:00.

B. 7:10.

C. 7:30.

D. 7:50.

7. A. The man should stay a little longer.

B. The man should leave at once.

C. The man will miss the train.

D. The man must try to catch the last train.

8. A. A furnished house.

B. A recent book.

C. A refinished cellar.

D. A new record.

9. A. She felt sorry for the man.

B. She had to pay the fine.

C. She couldn't accept the books.

D. She had to ask the man to pay for the overdue.

10. A. At 7:35.

B. At 7:45.

C. At 8:00.

D. At 7:15.

Section B

Directions: *In this section, you will hear three short passages. At the end of each passage, you will hear some questions. Both the passage and the questions will be spoken only once. After you hear a question, you must choose the best answer from the four choices marked A, B, C and D, and decide which is the best answer. Then mark the corresponding letter on the Answer Sheet with a single line through the center.*

Passage 1

Questions 11 to 13 are based on the passage you have just heard.

11. A. He lost consciousness.

    B. He was seriously injured.

    C. He was slightly wounded.

    D. He was buried under an icebox.

12. A. About four days.

    B. Around eight days.

    C. A day and a half.

    D. More than six days.

13. A. His father pulled him out in time.

    B. He left the area before the earthquake.

    C. He stayed in an icebox.

    D. Their house escaped the earthquake.

Passage 2

Questions 14 to 16 are based on the passage you have just heard.

14. A. Try out his new car.

    B. Avoid the police.

    C. Save Mrs. Smith.

    D. Avoid an accident.

15. A. He was speeding.

18

B. He was driving dangerously.

C. He was driving on a slippery road.

D. He was driving with expired license plates.

16. A. Nothing.

B. He was ordered to wait for their return.

C. He will lose his license.

D. He went with the police to the hospital.

Passage 3

Question 17 to 20 are based on the passage you have just heard.

17. A. It had many problems.

B. It was the most democratic country in the world.

C. It was fair to women.

D. It had some minor problems to solve.

18. A. The women of some states.

B. The members of the National Women's Association.

C. The woman in the state of Wyoming only.

D. The women in the state of Massachusetts only.

19. A. At the very beginning of the 20th Century.

B. At the end of the 19th Century.

C. After Susan Anthony's death.

D. Just before Susan Anthony's death.

20. A. She worked on the draft of the American Constitution.

B. She was the chairman of the National Women's Association.

C. She was born in New York and died in Massachusetts.

D. She was an activist in the women's movement for equal rights.

Section C

Directions: *In this section, you will hear a passage of about 150 words three times. The passage is printed on your Answer Sheet with about 10 words missing. First you will hear the whole passage from the beginning to the end just to get a general idea of it. Then, in the second reading, you will hear a signal indicating the beginning of a pause after each sentence, sometimes two* sentences or just part of a sentence. During the pause, you must write down the missing words you have just heard in the corresponding space on the Answer Sheet. There is also a different signal indicating the end of the pause. When you hear this signal, you must get ready for what comes next from the recording. You can check what you have written when the passage is read to you once again without the pauses.

A passage with 10 missing words

One of the __(21)__ of large modern cities is the number of big department stores, most of which are to be found in or near the __(22)__ area. They're vast buildings many stories high, where you can buy almost anything you need, from a box of toothpicks to a suite of __(23)__ . Most of them are very modern and are equipped with __(24)__ elevators and escalators, and have __(25)__ lighting, air-conditioning and ventilation. You can spend hours __(26)__ around in one of these department stores, and you will probably lose your way while you are doing so, in spite of the many __(27)__ pointing the way to the elevators and exits.

If you have been in one of these stores so long that you feel hungry, you and your family will not need to leave the building, for nearly all the big stores have cafes, snack bars or restaurants in them. __(28)__ , though occasionally an assistant may ask you whether he or she can be of help to you.

Another feature of Shanghai's shopping life is the chain-store, in which prices are lower than in the big store, and a wide variety of goods are offered — chiefly foodstuffs, household goods, clothing and stationery. __(29)__ , in spite of the vigilance of the store security guards.

A lot of the food stores in Shanghai now operate on the "serve yourself" system: __(30)__ . At the exit there are a number of counters where you pay for all your purchases together.

Part Three   Reading Comprehension

Directions: *In this section, there is a passage with 10 blanks. You are required to select one word for each blank from a list of choices given in a word bank following the passage. Read the passage through carefully before making your choices. Each choice in the bank is identified by a letter. Please mark the corresponding letter for each item on Answer Sheet with a single line* *through the center. **You may not use any of words in the bank more than once.***

A passage with 10 blanks

Years ago, doctors often said that pain was a normal part of life. In particular, when older patients   (31)   of pain, they were told it was a natural part of aging and they would have to learn to live with it.

Times have changed Today, we take pain   (32)   . Indeed, pain is now considered the fifth vital sign, as important as blood pressure, temperature, breathing rate and pulse in   (33)   a person's well-being. We know that chronic (慢性的) pain can disrupt (扰乱) a person's life, causing problems that   (34)   from missed work to depression.

That's why a growing number of hospitals now depend upon physicians who   (35)   in pain medicine. Not only do we evaluate the cause of the pain, which can help us treat the pain better, but we also help provide comprehensive therapy for depression and other psychological and social   (36)   related to chronic pain. Such comprehensive therapy often   (37)   the work of social workers, psychiatrists (心理医生) and psychologists, as well as specialists in pain medicine.

This modern   (38)   for pain management has led to a wealth of innovative treatments which are more effective and with fewer side effects than ever before. Decades ago, there were only a   (39)   number of drugs available, and many of them caused   (40)   side effects in older people, including dizziness(眩晕) and fatigue. This created a double-edged sword: the medications helped relieve the pain but caused other problems that could be worse than the pain itself.

A. result	E. relieved	I. Determining	M. respect
B. involves	F. issues	J. limited	N. prompting
C. significant	G. seriously	K. gravely	O. specialize
D. range	H. magnificent	L. complained	

Section B

Directions: *There are 2 passages in this section. Each passage is followed by some questions or unfinished statements. For each of them there are four choices marked A, B, C and D. You should decide on the best choice and mark the corresponding letter on Answer Sheet with a single line through the center.*

Passage 1

Questions 41 to 45 are based on the following passage.

In tese days of technological triumphs, it is well to remind ourselves from time to time living mechanisms(结构) are often incomparably more efficient than their artificial imitations. There is no better illustration of this idea than the sonar system of bats. It is billions of times more efficient and more sensitive than the radars and sonars designed by man.

Of course, the bats have had some 50 million years of evolution to refine their sonar. Their physiological mechanisms for echo(回声) location, based on all this accumulated experience, therefore merit out thorough study and analysis.

To appreciate the precision of the bat's echo location, we must first consider the degree of their reliance upon it. Thanks to sonar, an inset-eating bat can get along perfectly well without eyesight. This was brilliantly demonstrated by the Italian naturalist Lazzaro Spallanzani. He caught some bats in a bell tower, and on examining their stomaches' contents Spallanzani found that they had been able to capture and eat flying insects. We know from experiments that bats easily find insects in the dark of night, even when the insects make no sound that can be heard by human ears. A bat will catch hundreds of soft-bodied, silent-flying insects in a single hour. It will even detect and chase pebbles(卵石) tossed into the air.

41. According to the author, the sonar system of bats is an example of the idea that
_____ .

   A. this is the age of technological triumphs

   B. modern machines are inefficient

   C. living mechanisms are often more efficient than man-made machines

   D. artificial imitations are always less efficient than living mechanisms

42. The author suggests that the sonar system of bats _____ .

   A. was at the height of its perfection 50 million years ago

   B. is better than man-made sonar because it has had 50 million years to be refined

   C. should have been discovered by man many years ago

   D. is the same as it was 50 million years ago

43. Spallanzani's proof that bats could "see" in the dark was that _____ .

22

A. the bats found their way back to the bell tower

B. they found their way to their feeding area

C. only one of the bats starved to death

D. their stomachs contained bodies of insects

44. This article was written to illustrate _____ .

A. the deficiencies of man-made sonar

B. the dependence of man upon animals

C. that we are living in a machine age

D. that the sonar system of bats is remarkable

45. Which of the following is the main point of the article?

A. A bat will catch hundreds of insects in a single hour.

B. There is a perfection in nature which sometimes cannot be matched by man's creative efforts.

C. The phrase "blind as a bat" is valid.

D. Sonar and radar systems of man are inefficient.

Passage 2

Questions 46 to 50 are based on the following passage.

Sign has become a scientific hot button. Only in the past 20 years have specialists in language study realized that signed languages are unique— a speech of the hand They offer a new way to probe (调查) how the brain generates and understands language, and throw new light on an old scientific controversy: whether language, complete with grammar, is something that we are born with, or whether it is a learned behavior. The current interest in sign language has roots in the pioneering work of one rebel teacher at Gallaudet University in Washington, D.C. , the world's only liberal arts university for deaf people.

When Bill Stokoe went to Gallaudet to teach English, the school enrolled him in a course in signing. But Stokoe noticed something odd: among themselves, students signed differently from his classroom teacher.

Stokoe had been taught a sort of gestural code, each movement of the hands representing a word in English. At the time, American Sign Language (ASL) was thought to be no more than a form of pidgin English (混杂英语). But Stokoe believed the "hand talk" his students used looked richer. He wondered: Might deaf people actually have a genuine language? And could that language be unlike any other on Earth? It was 1955, when even deaf people dismissed their signing as "substandard". Stokoe's idea was academic heresy (异端邪说).

It is 37 years later, Stokoe — now devoting his time to writing and editing books and journals and to producing video materials on ASL and the deaf culture — is having lunch at a cafe near the Gallaudet campus and explaining how he started a revolution. For decades educators fought his idea that signed languages are natural languages like English, French and Japanese. They assumed language must be based on speech, the modulation (调节) of sound But sign language is based on the movement of hands, the modulation of space. "What I said," Stokoe explains, "is that language is not mouth stuff- it's brain stuff".

46. The study of sign language is thought to be _____ .

   A. an approach to simplifying the grammatical structure of a language

   B. an attempt to clarify misunderstanding about the origin of language

   C. a challenge to traditional views on the nature of language

   D. a new way to look at the learning of language

47. The present growing interest in sign language was stimulated by _____ .

   A. a leading specialist in the study of liberal arts

   B. an English teacher in a university for the deaf

   C. some senior experts in American Sign Language

   D. a famous scholar in the study of the human brain

48. According to Stokoe, sign language is _____ .

   A. an international language

   B. a substandard language

   C. an artificial language

   D. a genuine language

49. Most educators objected to Stokoe's idea because they thought _____ .

   A. a language should be easy to use and understand

   B. sign language was too artificial to be widely accepted

   C. a language could only exist in the form of speech sounds

   D. sign language was not extensively used even by deaf people

50. Stokoe's argument is based on his belief that _____ .

A. language is a product of the brain

B. language is a system of meaningful codes

C. sign language is derived from natural language

D. sign language is as efficient as any other language

Part Four Vocabulary

Directions: *Fou this part you are required to choose the best answer from A , B , C and D to complete the following sentences.*

51. She _____ her trip to New York because she was ill.

A. called off   B. put up   C. closed down   D. went off

52. _____ the storm, the ship would have reached its destination on time.

A. But for   B. In spite of   C. In case of   D. Because of

53. Don't _____ . I can help you with the typing.

A. matter   B. care   C. worry   D. concern

54. I hope they _____ this road by the time we come back next summer.

A. have repaired   B. will repair   C. are to repair   D. will have repaired

55. I suffered from mental _____ Because of stress from my job.

A. damage   B. relief   C. release   D. fatigue

56. It's high time we _____ something to stop road accidents.

A. did   B. are doing   C. will do   D. do

57. You will not be _____ about your food in time of great hunger.

A. special   B. peculiar   C. particular   D. specific

58. Crime is increasing worldwide, and there is every reason to believe the _____ will continue into the next decade.

A. emergency   B. pace   C. trend   D. schedule

59. You shouldn't have written in the _____ since the book belongs to the library.

A. interval   B. border   C. margin   D. edge

60. The _____ of airplane engines announced a coming air raid.

A. roar   B. exclamation   C. whistle   D. scream

61. This ticket _____ you to a free boat tour on the lake.

A. entities   B. appoints   C. grants   D. credits

62. This is the nurse who _____ to me when I was ill in hospital.

A. accompanied   B. attended   C. entertained   D. shielded

63. I think you have talked too much; what you need now is more action and _____ talk.

  A. few   B. less   C. fewer   D. little

64. The advertisement says this material doesn't _____ in the wash, but it has.

  A. contract   B. shrink   C. slim   D. dissolve

65. He was proud of being chosen to participate in the game and he _____ us that he would try as hard as possible.

  A. insured   B. assumed   C. guaranteed   D. assured

66. Does everyone on earth have an equal right _____ an equal share of its resources?

  A. to   B. at   C. by   D. over

67. The British are not so familiar with different cultures and other ways of doing things, _____ is often the case in other countries.

  A. so   B. what   C. as   D. that

68. We need a chairman _____ .

  A. for whom everyone has confidence   B. who everyone has confidence
  C. in whom everyone has confidence   D. whom everyone has confidence on

69. I hope that you'll be more careful in typing the letter. Don't _____ anything.

  A. lack   B. withdraw   C. omit   D. leak

70. The tomato juice left brown _____ on the front of my jacket.

  A. spot   B. point   C. track   D. trace

Part Five   Short Answer Questions

Directions: *In this part there is a short passage with five questions or incomplete statements. Read the passage carefully. Then answer the questions or complete the statement in the fewest possible words.*

Questions 71 to 75 are based on the passage.

  Chronic disability is affecting people more frequently at younger and younger age. According to the National Center for Health Statistics, the percentage of children under 17 years of age who are limited in activity due to chronic conditions increased by 86% from 1967 to 1979.

  Mental disease is affecting more and more people. The National Institute of Mental Health estimated in 1984 that one in every five Americans had a mental disorder. This

26

same study revealed that, during a six-month period, 8.3% of Americans suffered from an anxiety disorder, 6.4% had an alcohol or drug problem, and 6% had a mood disorder.

In addition to these various trends, one of the more significant facts that will affect the future of health care is that a large percentage of the population will be over 65 years old According to projections by the U. S. Bureau of the Census, the size of the American population over 65 in 1985 will have doubled by 2030.

Futurists generally assume that twenty-first century medicine will include new and more powerful drugs and various innovative technological interventions. However, futurists tend to ignore the serious problem presently arising from conventional medications. According to 1986 statistics, the average American receives 7.5 prescriptions a year. This is a particularly frightening number because we all know people who have not been prescribed any medications in the past year, which means that someone else is getting their 7.5 drugs.

71. Chronic disability has _____ among teenagers.

72. Anxiety disorder, alcohol or drug problem are considered to be _____ disease.

73. According to the passage, futurists should _____ attention to the problems arising from conventional medications.

74. It can be inferred from the statistics that a number of people have taken _____ than the average.

75. This passage _____ health problem.

Part Six Translation

Directions: *Finish the sentences on Answer Sheet by translating into English.*

76. Today the public is much concerned about the way _____ (大自然正被破坏).

77. _____ (汤姆已是个成熟的小伙子)who no longer depends on his parents for decision.

78. _____ (在工作日全家都忙着干活), but when the weekend came they loved to get in the car and drive around the nearby countryside.

79. Foreign bankers are cautiously optimistic _____ (国家经济的未来).

80. _____ (要不是他们的帮助), we shouldn't have succeeded.

Answer Sheet

Part One   Writing

A letter to a Schoolmate

_____

_____

_____

_____

_____

_____

_____

_____

_____

_____

_____

_____

_____

_____

_____

_____

_____

_____

_____

_____

_____

Part Two Listening Comprehension

Section A

1. [A][B][C][D]   2. [A][B][C][D]   3. [A][B][C][D]   4. [A][B][C][D]
5. [A][B][C][D]   6. [A][B][C][D]   7. [A][B][C][D]   8. [A][B][C][D]
9. [A][B][C][D]   10. [A][B][C][D]

Section B

11. [A][B][C][D] 12. [A][B][C][D]   13. [A][B][C][D]   14. [A][B][C][D]
15. [A][B][C][D] 16. [A][B][C][D]   17. [A][B][C][D]   18. [A][B][C][D]
19. [A][B][C][D] 20. [A][B][C][D]

Section C

21. _____   22. _____   23. _____   24. _____
25. _____   26. _____   27. _____
28. _____

_____
29. _____

_____
30. _____

_____

Part Three Reading Comprehension

Section A   Section B

31. [A][B][C][D][E][F][G][H][I][J][K][L][M][N][O]   41. [A][B][C][D]
32. [A][B][C][D][E][F][G][H][I][J][K][L][M][N][O]   42. [A][B][C][D]
33. [A][B][C][D][E][F][G][H][I][J][K][L][M][N][O]   43. [A][B][C][D]
34. [A][B][C][D][E][F][G][H][I][J][K][L][M][N][O]   44. [A][B][C][D]
35. [A][B][C][D][E][F][G][H][I][J][K][L][M][N][O]   45. [A][B][C][D]
36. [A][B][C][D][E][F][G][H][I][J][K][L][M][N][O]   46. [A][B][C][D]
37. [A][B][C][D][E][F][G][H][I][J][K][L][M][N][O]   47. [A][B][C][D]
38. [A][B][C][D][E][F][G][H][I][J][K][L][M][N][O]   48. [A][B][C][D]

39. [A][B][C][D][E][F][G][H][I][J][K][L][M][N][O] 49. [A][B][C][D]
40. [A][B][C][D][E][F][G][H][I][J][K][L][M][N][O] 50. [A][B][C][D]

Part Four Vocabulary

51. [A][B][C][D] 52. [A][B][C][D] 53. [A][B][C][D] 54. [A][B][C][D]
55. [A][B][C][D] 56. [A][B][C][D] 57. [A][B][C][D] 58. [A][B][C][D]
59. [A][B][C][D] 60. [A][B][C][D] 61. [A][B][C][D] 62. [A][B][C][D]
63. [A][B][C][D] 64. [A][B][C][D] 65. [A][B][C][D] 66. [A][B][C][D]
67. [A][B][C][D] 68. [A][B][C][D] 69. [A][B][C][D] 70. [A][B][C][D]

Part Five Short Answer Questions

71. Chronic disability has _____ among teenagers.

72. Anxiety disorder, alcohol or drug problem are considered to be _____ disease.

73. According to the passage, futurists should _____ attention to the problems arising from conventional medications.

74. It can inferred from the statistics that a number of people have taken than the average.

75. This passage _____ health problem.

Part Six Translation

76. _____
77. _____
78. _____
79. _____
80. _____

Model Test 3

Part One   Writing

Directions: *For this part, you are allowed thirty minutes to write a composition on the topic **Sandstorms**. You should write at least 120 words and you should base your composition on the outline (given in Chinese) below:*

1. 目前我国有些地区沙尘暴越来越严重;
2. 造成这种现象的原因;
3. 如何解决这一问题。

Part Two   Listening Comprehension

Section A

Directions: *In this section you will hear 10 short conversations. At the end of each conversation, a question will be asked about what was said, both the conversation and the question will be spoken only once. After each question there will be a pause. During the pause, you must read the four choices marked A, B, C and D, and decide which is the best answer. Then mark the corresponding letter on the Answer sheet with a single line through the center.*

1. A. Tom survived a traffic accident.

   B. Tom was killed in a traffic accident.

   C. Tom was knocked down by a car.

   D. Tom's car was accidentally lost.

2. A. She showed little interest in ancient costume.

   B. She found the show fascinating.

   C. She found the costume on display very good.

D. She had spent many hours at the show.

3. A. $ 1.40.

   B. $ 4.30.

   C. $ 6.40.

   D. $ 8.60.

4. A. Something went wrong with the bus.

   B. She took somebody to hospital.

   C. Something prevented her from catching the bus.

   D. She walked on foot instead of taking a bus.

5. A. He does not like it at all.

   B. He prefers symphony to folk music.

   C. He likes folk music ore than symphony.

   D. He likes folk music as much as symphony.

6. A. He has no time to make friends.

   B. He does not like his new job.

   C. He has adapted easily to his new job.

   D. He feels lonely now.

7. A. He has to do a lot of work.

   B. There will be a lot of people and cars on the streets.

   C. It's going to rain on Saturday.

   D. He does not like touring.

8. A. She is surprised to meet Jack.

   B. She has not seen Jack recently.

   C. She and Jack are close friends.

   D. Jack has changed a lot.

9. A. He didn't go to the interview.

   B. He succeeded in the interview.

   C. He forgot about the interview.

   D. He was too nervous in the interview.

10. A. She is sure who is going to win.

    B. Now it's a good time to start the game.

    C. The game has been going on for a long time.

    D. The same team always wins.

Section B

Directions: *In this section, you will hear three short passages. At the end of each passage, you will hear some questions. Both the passage and the questions will be spoken only once. After you hear a question, you must choose the best answer from the four choices marked A, B, C and D, and decide which is the best answer. Then mark the corresponding letter on the Answer Sheet with a single line through the center.*

Passage 1

Questions 11 to 13 are based on the passage you have just heard.

11. A. Because it takes too long to process all the applications.

    B. Because it is a library for special purposes.

    C. Because its resources are limited.

    D. Because there is a shortage of staff.

12. A. Discard his application form.

    B. Forbid him to borrow any items.

    C. Ask him to apply again.

    D. Cancel his video card.

13. A. One week.

    B. One month.

    C. Two weeks.

    D. Two months.

Passage 2

Questions 14 to 16 are based on the passage you have just heard.

14. A. They liked travelling.

    B. The reasons are unknown.

    C. They were driven out of their homes.

    D. They wanted to find a better place to live in.

15. A. They are unfriendly to Gypsies.

    B. They are envious of Gypsies.

    C. They admire the musical talent of the Gypsies.

D. They try to put up with Gypsies.

16. A. They are now taught in their own language.

B. They are now allowed to attend local schools.

C. Special schools have been set up for them.

D. Permanent homes have been built for them.

Passage 3

Questions 17 to 20 are based on the passage you have just heard.

17. A. Modern technology is now making towns in developing countries free of loud noise.

B. The increase in noise is a problem which cannot yet be solved by modern technology.

C. Gradual noise over a long period may have just as harmful an effect as loud or sudden noise.

D. There is no real solution to the problem of increasing noise in modern.

18. A. Noise made by people.

B. Noise made by machines.

C. Noise made by heavy traffic.

D. Noise made by airplanes.

19. A. Making us feel exciting.

B. Making us become nervous wrecks.

C. Damaging our hearing.

D. Spoiling the environment.

20. A. New silencing mechanisms are being designed.

B. New cure is experimented to solve the hearing problem.

C. Sound is forbidden in the city.

D. Some factories must be closed.

Section C

Directions: *In this section, you will hear a passage of about 150 words three times. The passage is printed on your Answer Sheet with about 10 words missing. First you will hear the whole passage from the beginning to the end just to get a general idea of it. Then, in the second reading, you will hear a sig-*

nal indicating the beginning of a pause after each sentence, sometimes two sentences or just part of a sentence. During the pause, you must write down the missing words you have just heard in the corresponding space on the Answer Sheet. There is also a different signal indicating the end of the pause. When you hear this signal, you must get ready for what comes next from the recording. You can check what you have written when the passage is read to you once again without the pauses.

A passage with 10 missing words

Do you have ____(21)____ sleeping at night? Then, maybe, this is for you:

When you worry about not being able to sleep and ____(22)____ around, trying to find a ____(23)____ position, you're probably only making matters ____(24)____ . What happens is that your heart rate actually ____(25)____ , making it more difficult to ____(26)____ . You may also have some bad habits that contribute to the problem. Do you rest ____(27)____ during the day? Do you get almost no exercise or do you exercise strenuously late in the day? Do you think about sleep a lot or sleep late on the weekend?

Any of all these factors might be leading to your insomnia by disrupting your body's natural rhythm. What should you do then on those sleepless nights? Don't bother with sleeping pills. ____(28)____ . The best thing to do is to drink some milk or eat some cheese or tuna fish. ____(29)____ . This will enable you to relax and you'll be on the way to get a good night's sleep. ____(30)____ . Think about this: when the morning comes, everything will be all right again.

Part Three   Reading Comprehension

Directions: *In this section, there is a passage with 10 blanks. You are required to select one word for each blank from a list of choices given in a word bank following the passage. Read the passage through carefully before making your choices. Each choice in the bank is identified by a letter. Please mark the corresponding letter for each item on Answer Sheet with a single line through the center.* **You may not use any of words in the bank more than once.**

A passage with 10 blanks

The use of nuclear power has already spread all over the world However, scientists still have not agreed on what should be done with the large amounts of waste material that keep increasing every year.

Most waste materials are __(31)__ of simply by placing them somewhere. But nuclear waste must be __(32)__ with extremely great care. It gives off dangerous radiation and it will continue to be __(33)__ for hundreds, thousands, even millions of years.

How should we get rid of such waste material in such a way that it will not harm the __(34)__? Where can we possibly __(35)__ Distribute it? One idea is to put this radioactive waste inside a thick container, which is then dropped to the bottom of the ocean. But some scientists believe that this way of __(36)__ nuclear waste could kill fish and other living things in the oceans or __(37)__ with their growth. Another way to __(38)__ nuclear waste is to send it into space, to the sun, where it would be burned. Other scientists suggest that this polluting material should be __(39)__ thousands of meters under the earth's surface. Such underground areas must be __(40)__ of possible earthquakes. Advances are being made. But it may still be many years before this problem could be finally settled.

A. free	E. deadly	I. remove	M. environment
B. interfere	F. safely	J. dealt	N. disturb
C. residence	G. buried	K. disposed	O. unfavorable
D. handled	H. scattering	L. discarding	

Section B

Directions: *There are 2 passages in this section. Each passage is followed by some questions or unfinished statements. For each of them there are four choices marked A, B, C and D. You should decide on the best choice and mark the corresponding letter on Answer Sheet with a single line through the center.*

Passage 1

Questions 41 to 45 are based on the following passage.

People landing at London's Heathrow airport have something new to look at as they fly over Britain's capital city. It is attractive, simple and a little strange. The Millennium Dome is a huge semi-circle of plastic and steel and it contains the largest public space in the world. It has been built to house an exhibition of all that is best in British life, learning and leisure.

The Millennium Dome was designed by Sir Richard Rogers, one of Britain's most famous architects. **His work points the way to new developments in building**. Think of it as a giant symbol of the buildings in which we will all be living and working in the near future.

Buildings are also a part of history. They express the culture of the times. Sir Richard Rogers is aware of this responsibility. While different designers have individual styles, their work also has a common style. That is: to express the values of the information age.

What is an "information age" Building? The dome is a good example. After the Millennium exhibition ends, it will be used for anther purpose. Just as people no longer have "jobs for life", modern buildings are designed for a number of different uses.

Another Richard Roger's building, the Pompidou Center in France, uses the idea that information is communication. Instead of being hidden in the walls, heating pipes and elevators are open to public view. The Pompidou Center is a very honest building. It tells you how it works.

41. The Millennium Dome has been originally built to hold an exhibition _____ .

    A. of different building designs

    B. of everything that can draw the attention of people

    C. of the finest things in Britain

    D. of recent developments in information technology

42. Sir Richard Rogers clearly knows that it is his duty to _____.

    A. create something out of a unique style

    B. house those people who will often change their jobs

    C. make his buildings historic ones

    D. construct a building that can meet the changes of the modern age

43. The sentence "His work points the way to new developments in building" (Line 2, Para. 2) implies that the designer Sir Richard Rogers _____.

    A. has developed a new set of building standards

    B. strictly follows the tradition in his work

    C. is a pioneer architect of his age

    D. is the father of modern architecture

44. The Pompidou Center in France is outstanding in the fact that _____.

    A. people in it are able to visit each other conveniently

B. visitors can see clearly the structure and facilities of the whole building

C. it makes use of the best techniques invented in the information age

D. it was designed and built by an honest British designer

45. This short passage mainly tells us about _____ .

A. the unique contribution of a famous architect

B. modern buildings of various styles

C. a few developments in house-building

D. the common features of British and French buildings

Passage 2

Questions 46 to 50 are based on the following passage.

The sense of sound is one of our most important means of knowing what is going on around us. Sound has a wasted product, too, in the form of noise. Noise has been called unwanted sound. Noise is growing and it may get much worse before it gets any better.

Scientists, for several years, have been studying how noise affects people and animals. They are surprised by what they have learned. Peace and quiet are becoming harder to find Noise pollution is a threat that should be looked at carefully.

There is a saying about it being so noisy that you can't hear yourself think. Doctors who study noise believe that we must sometimes hear ourselves think. If we don't we may have headaches, other aches and pains. Or even worse mental problems.

Noise adds more tension to a society that already faces enough stress.

But noise is not a new problem. In ancient Rome, people complained so much about noise that the government stopped chariots from moving through the streets at night!

Ways of making less noise are now being tested. There are even laws controlling noise. We cannot return to the "good old days" of peace and quiet. But we can reduce noise if we shout loudly enough about it.

46. Why are scientists surprised by the findings in their noise study?

A. Because the world is becoming more and more noisy.

B. Because they have learned that noise is also a kind of pollution.

C. Because noise is an unwanted waste for human beings.

D. Because people knew little about the danger of noise before.

47. What may be the result if we cannot hear ourselves think?

A. We may forget what we have thought about

B. Our thoughts may be interfered.

C. Our mind may be harmed.

D. We may have difficulty using the right words.

48. When the writer says we cannot return to the good old days, he means that _____.

A. our society is becoming much worse than before

B. in our modern society it is hard to lead a quiet life

C. the old days were much happier than the present time

D. it is impossible for us to deal with noise as we did before

49. From the last sentence of the passage we can learn that _____.

A. we can put noise under control if our measures are effective

B. sometimes we have to shout loudly so that others can hear us

C. shouting is a chief cause of noise pollution

D. it is important to warn people of the danger of noise pollution

50. Which of the following statements is TRUE according to the passage?

A. Only recently did people realize the harmfulness of noise.

B. Noise pollution is the worst kind of pollution we suffer from.

C. People are now trying to find ways to make noise as low as possible.

D. The writer thinks that it is almost impossible for people to avoid noise.

Part Four   Vocabulary

Directions: *Fou this part you are required to choose the best answer from A , B , C and D to complete the following sentences.*

51. This kind of medicine has the power to _____ poison.

A. splash   B. resist   C. adopt   D. occupy

52. He is easily _____ so I do not like to talk with him.

A. defended   B. afforded   C. created   D. offended

53. I am _____ to believe that he won't come back to see his wife again.

A. inclined   B. puzzled

C. accompanied   D. performed

54. Before you mail this letter, you should check again whether you have _____ it or

not.

A. sunk   B. sighed   C. sought   D. sealed

55. After talking for nearly ten hours, he _____ to the government's pressure at last.

A. expressed   B. yielded   C. decreased   D. approved

56. My hands and feet were _____ with cold as I waited for the bus.

A. cliff   B. still   C. stiff   D. stick

57. This problem is beyond his ability and he can not _____ it.

A. slip   B. pack   C. gain   D. solve

58. When you buy the spare parts for your car, try to get the _____ ones from the authorized dealer.

A. genuine   B. generous   C. genius   D. gentle

59. If you use _____ , you can get a higher quality picture.

A. wax   B. shame   C. goose   D. slides

60. Who _____ this country, the people or the president? This question is not easy to answer.

A. frightens   B. differs   C. displays   D. governs

61. This year our university does not have any _____ to continue the international student exchange program.

A. function   B. fundamental   C. funeral   D. funds

62. Who is the patient being _____ on?

A. painted   B. operated   C. tied   D. fetched

63. Mary is _____ of music but I am not.

A. pause   B. adventure   C. grammatical   D. fond

64. This man has been proved _____ of murder.

A. guilty   B. spoil   C. flash   D. curious

65. The international situation is very _____ in the Middle East.

A. delicious   B. perfect   C. delicate   D. percent

66. Even though he knew that I should study, he still _____ me to go to the movies.

A. recognized   B. extended

C. persuaded   D. unexpected

67. We _____ that it will take another four months to finish this plan.

A. grant   B. estimate   C. council   D. check

68. He read the paper several times but he still _____ some printer's errors.

A. overlooked   B. ignored   C. noticed   D. outlined

40

69. She often talks with a _____ appearance but in fact she is always telling lies.

   A. tidy   B. sincere   C. worship   D. merry

70. If the students can not support themselves during their study in university, they may ask for a student _____ from the government.

   A. menu   B. spoon   C. loan   D. bond

Part Five   Short Answer Questions

Directions: *In this part there is a short passage with five questions or incomplete statements. Read the passage carefully. Then answer the questions or complete the statement in the fewest possible words.*

Questions 71 to 75 are based on the passage.

The first airliner to use the new jet engines was built in Britain and it began carrying passengers in 1952. It had two jet engines and flew much higher than petrol-engined airliner. At this height, the air is thinner and very cold, and so the aeroplane can cut through the air more easily. There are no clouds to disturb the flight of the airliner, and rain and thunderstorms are far below it. The sky above is a bright blue.

However, because the air is so cold and thin, the cabin has to be air-conditioned and has to be at normal pressure so that the passengers may eat, read and sleep in comfort.

Today, all long distance airliners have jet engines. The modern jet airliners are very big and carry as many as 200 passengers. Some airliners are even bigger: they can carry 350 passengers on two different floors. In this way, air travel can be made much cheaper.

Tomorrow's airliners will be flying at twice the speed of today's airliners. In fact, a new-type airliner has already reached this enormous speed. It can carry passengers in safety and comfort high up in the blue sky.

71. England made the first _____ which used the new jet engines in 1952.

72. Thanks to its height, the jet airliner can go through the air _____ .

73. With the air conditioning and regular pressure in the cabin, the passengers can stay inside _____ .

74. The expenses of air travel will go down greatly, if some airliners can carry 350 passengers on two different _____ .

75. The writer of the text believes that the aeroplane industry has a _____ future.

Part Six   Translation

Directions: *Finish the sentences on Answer Sheet by translating into English.*

76. Although the professor had explained this point in great detail, _____(但许多学生仍然不理解).

77. _____(无论他如何努力), he just couldn't understand higher mathematics.

78. She treated the little boy very kindly, _____ (好像她是他妈妈).

79. The two pictures are similar, at least _____ (就背景颜色而言).

80. _____ (抓住这次机会),and I promise you won't regret it.

Answer Sheet

Part One   Writing

Sandstorms

_____

_____

_____

_____

_____

_____

_____

_____

_____

_____

_____

_____

_____

_____

_____

_____

_____

_____

_____

_____

Part Two Listening Comprehension

Section A

1. [A][B][C][D]   2. [A][B][C][D]   3. [A][B][C][D]   4. [A][B][C][D]

5. [A][B][C][D]   6. [A][B][C][D]   7. [A][B][C][D]   8. [A][B][C][D]

9. [A][B][C][D]   10. [A][B][C][D]

Section B

11. [A][B][C][D] 12. [A][B][C][D] 13. [A][B][C][D] 14. [A][B][C][D]

15. [A][B][C][D] 16. [A][B][C][D] 17. [A][B][C][D] 18. [A][B][C][D]

19. [A][B][C][D] 20. [A][B][C][D]

Section C

21. _____   22. _____   23. _____   24. _____   25. _____

26. _____   27. _____   28. _____

29. _____

_____

30. _____

_____

Part Three Reading Comprehension

Section A

31. [A][B][C][D][E][F][G][H][I][J][K][L][M][N][O]

32. [A][B][C][D][E][F][G][H][I][J][K][L][M][N][O]

33. [A][B][C][D][E][F][G][H][I][J][K][L][M][N][O]

34. [A][B][C][D][E][F][G][H][I][J][K][L][M][N][O]

35. [A][B][C][D][E][F][G][H][I][J][K][L][M][N][O]

36. [A][B][C][D][E][F][G][H][I][J][K][L][M][N][O]

37. [A][B][C][D][E][F][G][H][I][J][K][L][M][N][O]

38. [A][B][C][D][E][F][G][H][I][J][K][L][M][N][O]

39. [A][B][C][D][E][F][G][H][I][J][K][L][M][N][O]

40. [A][B][C][D][E][F][G][H][I][J][K][L][M][N][O]

Section B

41. [A][B][C][D]

42. [A][B][C][D]

43. [A][B][C][D]

44. [A][B][C][D]

45. [A][B][C][D]

46. [A][B][C][D]

47. [A][B][C][D]

48. [A][B][C][D]

49. [A][B][C][D]

50. [A][B][C][D]

Part Four Vocabulary

51. [A][B][C][D] 52. [A][B][C][D] 53. [A][B][C][D] 54. [A][B][C][D]
55. [A][B][C][D] 56. [A][B][C][D] 57. [A][B][C][D] 58. [A][B][C][D]
59. [A][B][C][D] 60. [A][B][C][D] 61. [A][B][C][D] 62. [A][B][C][D]
63. [A][B][C][D] 64. [A][B][C][D] 65. [A][B][C][D] 66. [A][B][C][D]
67. [A][B][C][D] 68. [A][B][C][D] 69. [A][B][C][D] 70. [A][B][C][D]

Part Five Short Answer Questions

71. England made the first _____ which used the new jet engines in 1952.
72. Thanks to its height, the jet airliner can go through the air _____ .
73. With the air conditioning and regular pressure in the cabin, the passengers can stay inside _____ .
74. The expenses of air travel will go down greatly, if some airliners can carry 350 passengers on two different _____ .
75. The writer of the text believes that the aeroplane industry has a _____ future.

Part Six Translation

76. _____
77. _____
78. _____
79. _____
80. _____

Model Test 4

Part One   Writing

Directions: *For this part*, *you are allowed thirty minutes to write a composition on the topic* **Practice Makes Perfect**. *You should write at least 100 words*, *and base your composition on the outline* (*given in Chinese*) *below*:

1. 怎样理解"熟能生巧"？
2. 例如：在英语学习中……
3. 又如……

Part Two   Listening Comprehension

Section A

Directions: *In this section you will hear 10 short conversations*. *At the end of each conversation*, *a question will be asked about what was said*, *both the conversation and the question will be spoken only once*. *After each question there will be a pause*. *During the pause*, *you must read the four choices marked A*, *B*, *C and D*, *and decide which is the best answer*. *Then mark the corresponding letter on the Answer sheet with a single line through the center*.

1. A. Husband and wife.

   B. Son and mother.

   C. Patient and doctor.

   D. Teacher and student.

2. A. Close the window.

   B. Put on more clothes.

   C. Take a deep breath.

D. Move to another room.

3. A. The man has changed his destination.

   B. The man is returning his ticket.

   C. The man is flying to New York tomorrow morning.

   D. The man can't manage to go to New York as planned.

4. A. She does not think painting the walls is necessary.

   B. He wants their walls to be painted in a darker color.

   C. He wants their walls to be painted in a lighter color.

   D. He does not like white color.

5. A. Servant and hostess.

   B. Waiter and customer.

   C. Doorkeeper and visitor.

   D. Shop assistant and old customer.

6. A. Fifty-five minutes.

   B. Thirty-five minutes.

   C. Twenty-five minutes.

   D. Twenty minutes.

7. A. She does not need the job.

   B. She has not got a job yet.

   C. She has got a good job.

   D. She is going to start work soon.

8. A. 9:00.

   B. 10:30.

   C. 10:00.

   D. 9:30.

9. A. She rejects their request.

   B. She accepts their request.

   C. She agrees to consider their request.

   D. She asks them to come with others.

10. A. He would help her carry the luggage.

    B. He wouldn't help her carry the luggage.

    C. He had other things to do.

    D. He is glad to give her a hand.

Section B

Directions: *In this section, you will hear three short passages. At the end of each passage, you will hear some questions. Both the passage and the questions will be spoken only once. After you hear a question, you must choose the best answer from the four choices marked A, B, C and D, and decide which is the best answer. Then mark the corresponding letter on the Answer Sheet with a single line through the center.*

Passage 1

Questions 11 to 13 are based on the passage you have just heard.

11. A. They invited him to a party.

    B. They gave a special dinner for him.

    C. They asked him to make a speech.

    D. They invited his wife to attend the dinner.

12. A. He was embarrassed.

    B. He felt sad.

    C. He felt greatly encouraged.

    D. He was deeply touched.

13. A. Tom's wife did not think that the company was fair to Tom.

    B. Tom's wife was satisfied with the gold watch.

    C. Tom did not like the gold watch.

    D. The company had some financial problems.

Passage 2

Questions 14 to 16 are based on the passage you have just heard.

14. A. He missed the appointment.

    B. He was sick.

    C. He arrived late.

    D. He was very busy.

15. A. He was busy sightseeing.

    B. He couldn't reach Mr. Jordan's office.

    C. He didn't want to see Mr. Jordan any more.

D. He didn't want to take the trouble making it.

16. A. The trip didn't do any good to his health.

   B. The trip was a complete disappointment.

   C. The trip was repayable but not fruitful in terms of business.

   D. The trip made it possible for him to meet many interesting people.

Passage 3

Question 17 to 20 are based on the passage you have just heard

17. A. During the First World War.

   B. During the Second World War.

   C. During the Civil War.

   D. During the Gulf War.

18. A. She knew nothing about Wilson's secret.

   B. She was a policewoman.

   C. She was one of the secretaries of the War Office.

   D. She loved Wilson very much.

19. A. Because he could have time to send war information to the Germans.

   B. Because it was the best place to wait for his girlfriend during wartime.

   C. Because he needed time to plan for the parties.

   D. Because it was a quiet place to analyze war situation.

20. A. He had nothing to do with the Germans.

   B. He had been sending information to the Germans by playing piano.

   C. He was a spy planted by the German.

   D. He was a German.

Section C

Directions: *In this section, you will hear a passage of about 150 words three times. The passage is printed on your Answer Sheet with about 10 words missing. First you will hear the whole passage from the beginning to the end just to get a general idea of it. Then, in the second reading, you will hear a signal indicating the beginning of a pause after each sentence, sometimes two sentences or just part of a sentence. During the pause, you must write down the missing words you have just heard in the corresponding space on the An-*

swer Sheet. There is also a different signal indicating the end of the pause. When you hear this signal, you must get ready for what comes next from the recording. You can check what you have written when the passage is read to you once again without the pauses.

A passage with 10 missing words

Since the __(21)__ of history, men have gathered information and have __(22)__ to pass it on to other men. The __(23)__ of word-pictures on the walls of __(24)__ caves as well as hieroglyphics(象形文字) on stone tablets __(25)__ some of man's earliest efforts to __(26)__ information. Evidently, these efforts were very simple and __(27)__.

But as civilizations grew more complex, better methods of communication were needed. The written word, carrier pigeons, the telegraph and many other devices carried ideas faster and faster from man to man but still not fast enough to satisfy ever-growing needs. In recent years, as men entered the information epoch, a new type of machine, __(28)__. With the invention and development of computers, it is as if man has suddenly come upon Aladin's magic lamp.

__(29)__. For this reason, computers can be defined as devices which accept information, perform mathematical or logical operations with the input information, and then supply the results of these operations as new information.

__(30)__. However, although computers can replace men in dull, routine tasks, they only work according to the instructions given them, in other words, they have to be programmed. Their achievements are not very spectacular when compared to what the minds of men can do.

Part Three   Reading Comprehension

Directions: *In this section, there is a passage with 10 blanks. You are required to select one word for each blank from a list of choices given in a word bank following the passage. Read the passage through carefully before making your choices. Each choice in the bank is identified by a letter. Please mark the corresponding letter for each item on Answer Sheet with a single line through the center. **You may not use any of words in the bank more than once.***

A passage with 10 blanks

The biggest safety threat facing airlines today may not be a terrorist with a gun, but the man with the   (31)   computer in business class. In the last 15 years, pilots have reported well over 100   (32)   that could have been caused by electromagnetic interference. This source of the interference   (33)   unconfirmed, but increasingly, experts are pointing the blame at portable electronic device such as portable computers, radio and cassette players and mobile telephones.

RTCA, an organization which advises the aviation industry, has recommended that all airlines ban such devices from being used during   (34)   stages of flight,   (35)   take-off and landing. Some experts have gone further, calling for a total ban during all flights. Currently, rules on using these devices are left up to individual airlines. And although some airlines prohibit passengers from using such equipment during take-off and landing, most are   (36)   to enforce a total ban, given that many passengers want to work during flights.

The difficulty is   (37)   how electromagnetic fields might affect an aircraft's computers. Experts know that portable device emit radiation which   (38)   those wavelengths which aircraft use for navigation and communication. But, because they have not been able to reproduce these effects in a laboratory, they have no way of knowing whether the interference might be dangerous or not.

The fact that aircraft may be vulnerable to interference raises the risk that terrorists may use radio systems in order to damage navigation   (39)   . As worrying, though, is the passenger who can't hear the instructions to turn off his radio because the   music's too   (40)   .

Word Bank

A. definite	E. critical	I. portable	M. affects
B. incidents	F. particularly	J. enormous	N. equipment
C. effects	G. reluctant	K. predicting	O. loud
D. remains	H. refreshing	L. liberal	

Section B

Directions: *There are 2 passages in this section. Each passage is followed by some questions or unfinished statements. For each of them there are four choices*

51

Passage 1

Questions 41 to 45 are based on the following passage.

Today, there are many avenues open to those who wish to continue their education. However, nearly all require some break in one's career in order to attend school full time.

Part time education, that is, attending school at night or for one weekend a month, tends to drag the process out over time and puts the completion of a degree program out of reach of many people. Additionally, such programs require a fixed time commitment which can also impact negatively on one's career and family time.

Of the many approaches to teaching and learning, however, perhaps the most flexible and accommodating is that called distance learning. Distance learning is an educational method which allows the students the flexibility to study at his or her own pace to achieve the academic goals which are so necessary in today's world. The time required to study may be set aside at the student's convenience with due regard to all life's other requirements. Additionally, the student may enroll in distance learning courses from virtually any place in the world, while continuing to pursue their chosen career. Tutorial assistance may be available via regular airmail, telephone, facsimile machine, teleconferencing and over the Internet.

Good distance learning programs are characterized by the inclusion of a subject evaluation tool with every subject. This precludes the requirement for a student to travel away from home to take a test. Another characteristic of a good distance learning program is the equivalence of the distance learning course with the same subject materials as those students taking the course on the home campus. The resultant diploma or degree should also be the same whether distance learning or on-campus study is employed. The individuality of the professor/student relationship is another characteristic of a good distance learning program. In the final analysis, a good distance learning program has a place not only for the individual student but also the corporation or business that wants to work in partnership with their employees for the educational benefit, professional development, and business growth of the organization. Sponsoring distance learning programs for their employees gives the business the advantage of retaining career-minded people while contributing to their personal and professional growth through education.

41. According to the passage, which of the following is NOT a disadvantage of part time education?

    A. It requires some break in one's career.

    B. It tends to last too long for many people to complete a degree program.

    C. It affects one's career.

    D. It gives the student less time to share with the family.

42. Which of the following is NOT an advantage of distance learning?

    A. The student may choose his or her own pace.

    B. The student may study at any time to his or her convenience.

    C. They can pursue their chosen career while studying.

    D. Their tutorial assistance comes through regular airmail, telephone, facsimile machine, etc.

43. What benefit will distance learning program bring to a business?

    A. Recruitment of more talented people.

    B. Good image of the business.

    C. Better cooperation with universities.

    D. Further training of employees and business growth.

44. Good distance learning program have the following characteristic EXCEPT _____.

    A. that distance learning course is the same as students taking courses in campus

    B. that the result diploma or degree should be same as on campus study

    C. that professor-student relationship is strictly one to one all through the course

    D. that it includes subject evaluation tool

45. What benefit will distance learning bring to an employee of a business?

    A. Professional growth.

    B. Good relationship with the employer.

    C. Good impression on the employer.

    D. Higher salary.

Passage 2

Questions 46 to 50 are based on the following passage.

When one looks back upon the fifteen hundred years that are the life span of the English language, he should be able to notice a number of significant truths. The history of our language has always been a history of constant change—at times a slow, almost imperceptible(感觉不到的)change, at other times a violent collision between two languages. Our language has always been a living growing organism, it has never been static. Another significant truth that emerges from such a study is that language at all times has been the possession not of one class or group but of many. At one extreme it has been the property of the common, ignorant folk, who have used it in the daily business of their living, much as they have used their animals or the kitchen pots and pans. At the other extreme it has been the treasure of those who have respected it as an instrument and a sign of civilization, and who have struggled by writing it down to give it some permanence, order, dignity, and if possible, a little beauty.

As we consider our changing language, we should note here two developments that are of special and immediate importance to us. One is that since the time of the Anglo-Saxons there has been an almost complete reversal of the different devices for showing the relationship of words in a sentence. Anglo-Saxon (old English) was a language of many inflections. Modern English has few inflections. We must now depend largely on word order and function words to convey the meanings that the older language did by means of changes in the forms of words. Function words, you should understand, are words such as prepositions, conjunctions, and a few others that are used primarily to show relationships among other words. A few inflections, however, have survived. And when some word inflections come into conflict with word order, there may be trouble for the users of the language, as we shall see later when we turn our attention to such maters as WHO or WHOM and ME or I. The second fact we must consider is that as language itself changes, our attitudes toward language forms change also. The eighteenth century, for example, produced from various sources a tendency to fix the language into patterns not always set in and grew, until at the present time there is a strong tendency to restudy and re-evaluate language practices in terms of the ways in which people speak and write.

46. In contrast to the earlier linguists, modern linguists tend to _____.

   A. attempt to continue the standardization of the language

   B. evaluate language practices in terms of current speech rather than standards or
      proper patterns

   C. be more concerned about the improvement of the language than its analysis orhis-
      tory

   D. be more aware of the rules of the language usage

54

47. Choose the appropriate meaning for the word "inflection" used in line 5 of paragraph 2.

    A. Changes in the forms of words.

    B. Changes in sentence structures.

    C. Changes in spelling rules.

    D. Words that have similar meanings.

48. Which of the following statements is not mentioned in the passage?

    A. It is generally believed that the year 1500 can be set as the beginning of the modern English language.

    B. Some other languages had great influence on the English language at some stages of its development.

    C. The English language has been and still in a state of relatively constant change.

    D. Many classes or groups have contributed to the development of the English language.

49. The author of these paragraphs is probably a(an) _____.

    A. historian

    B. philosopher

    C. anthropologist

    D. linguist

50. Which of the following can be best used as the title of the passage?

    A. The history of the English language.

    B. Our changing attitude towards the English language.

    C. Our changing language.

    D. Some characteristics of modern English.

Part Four Vocabulary

Directions: *Fou this part you are required to choose the best answer from A,B,C and D to complete the following sentences.*

51. This is an _____ that will not be easily forgotten.

    A. impact   B. academic   C. insult   D. alternative

52. Please _____ me for my rudeness. I really do not know the custom here.

    A. engage   B. comfort   C. execute   D. forgive

53. Water and air are _____ to human beings. We can not live without them.

A. harbour   B. function   C. definite   D. essential

54. When the airplane takes off, the passengers are told to _____ their seat belts.

  A. fountain   B. fix   C. tight   D. fasten

55. This is not what we asked you to do. You can not get more pay for the _____
work.

  A. owing   B. device   C. tired   D. extra

56. My throat is _____ . I cannot speak any more.

  A. sore   B. purchase   C. glow   D. faint

57. Many years ago, a lot of factories were _____ from big cities to the mountainous
areas in case of war.

  A. transferred   B. transformed   C. transmitted   D. transported

58. He said in his letter that he would _____ some photographs but I couldn't find
anything in the envelope.

  A. case   B. double   C. enclose   D. nonsense

59. Many English words are _____ from Latin.

  A. displayed   B. spread   C. lost   D. derived

60. I feel _____ to say that I can not believe what he said.

  A. wanted   B. observed   C. obliged   D. wandered

61. His proposal is very _____ . We do not need any explanation.

  A. concrete   B. loyal   C. grey   D. draft

62. This is a _____ computer, which we just bought for our research.

  A. detective   B. luggage   C. digital   D. grave

63. The two pictures are _____ . We don't know which is the copy.

  A. identical   B. likely   C. limited   D. resemble

64. If you don't want to wash your jacket, you may send it to a _____ .

  A. participant   B. planet   C. laundry   D. ribbon

65. If the _____ in the test is too small, we can not get a good result.

  A. sample   B. percent   C. leisure   D. flight

66. Jack wants to be _____ when he grows up.

  A. a bar   B. a cousin   C. an opponent   D. an astronaut

67. This is a very big hotel and it can _____ more than 1,000 people.

  A. accommodate   B. display   C. faint   D. loaf

68. Professor Li _____ in doing his experiment for nearly ten years.

A. insisted   B. piled   C. persisted   D. split

69. The new plan is _____ and everybody present agrees with it.

A. feasible   B. adventure   C. appendix   D .camel

70. Please be _____. Your question is too general.

A. limited   B. narrow   C. specific   D. thorough

Part Five   Short Answer Questions

Directions: *In this part there is a short passage with five questions or incomplete state-*
ments. Read the passage carefully. Then answer the questions or complete
the statement in the fewest possible words.

Questions 71 to 75 are based on the passage.

Men cannot manufacture blood as efficiently as women can. This makes surgery riskier for men. Men also need more oxygen because they do not breathe as often as women. But men breathe more deeply and this exposes them to another risk. When the air is polluted, they draw more of it into their lungs.

A more recent — and chilling — finding is the effect of automobile and truck exhaust fumes on children's intelligence. These exhaust fumes are the greatest source of lead pollution in cities. Researchers have found that the children with the highest concentration of lead in their bodies have the lowest scores on intelligence tests and that boys score lower than girls. It is possible that these low scores are connected to the deeper breathing that is typical of the male.

Men's bones are larger than women's and they are arranged somewhat differently. The feminine walk that evokes so many whistles is a matter of bone structure. Men have broader shoulders and a narrower pelvis(骨盆), which enables them to stride out with no waste motion. A woman's wider pelvis, designed for child-bearing, forces her to put more movement into each step she takes with the result that she displays a bit of a jiggle and sway as she walks.

If you think a man is brave because he climbs a ladder to clean out of the roof gutters, don't forget that it is easier for him than for a woman. The angle at which a woman's thigh is joined to her knees makes climbing awkward for her, no matter whether it is a ladder or stairs or a mountain that she is tackling.

71. A proper topic for this passage may be _____.

72. Men suffer more from air pollution because they _____.

73. What makes men's walking different from women's? _____.

74. As far as body structures are concerned, _____ face more danger in climbing mountains.

75. How many differences between men and women are mentioned in this passage? _____.

Part Six   Translation

Directions: *Finish the sentences on Answer Sheet by translating into English.*

76. It's a sentimental value. _____ (它使我想起我的祖母).

77. He worked so hard that _____ (他提前一年获得博士学位).

78. _____ (既然李教授已答应出席会议), we'd like to request him to deliver a speech.

79. _____ (就我所知), they have been emotionally detached from each other for some time.

80. I haven't got any cash with me, _____ (但是我可以开支票).

Answer Sheet

Part One   Writing

Practice Makes Perfect

_____

_____

_____

_____

_____

_____

_____

_____

_____

_____

_____

_____

_____

_____

_____

_____

_____

_____

_____

_____

_____

_____

_____

Part Two   Listening Comprehension

Section A

1. [A][B][C][D]   2. [A][B][C][D]   3. [A][B][C][D]   4. [A][B][C][D]
5. [A][B][C][D]   6. [A][B][C][D]   7. [A][B][C][D]   8. [A][B][C][D]
9. [A][B][C][D]   10. [A][B][C][D]

Section B

11. [A][B][C][D]   12. [A][B][C][D]   13. [A][B][C][D]   14. [A][B][C][D]
15. [A][B][C][D]   16. [A][B][C][D]   17. [A][B][C][D]   18. [A][B][C][D]
19. [A][B][C][D]   20. [A][B][C][D]

Section C

21. _____   22. _____   23. _____   24. _____
25. _____   26. _____   27. _____
28. _____

_____

29. _____

_____

30. _____

_____

Part Three   Reading Comprehension

Section A   ### Section B

31. [A][B][C][D][E][F][G][H][I][J][K][L][M][N][O]   41. [A][B][C][D]
32. [A][B][C][D][E][F][G][H][I][J][K][L][M][N][O]   42. [A][B][C][D]
33. [A][B][C][D][E][F][G][H][I][J][K][L][M][N][O]   43. [A][B][C][D]
34. [A][B][C][D][E][F][G][H][I][J][K][L][M][N][O]   44. [A][B][C][D]
35. [A][B][C][D][E][F][G][H][I][J][K][L][M][N][O]   45. [A][B][C][D]
36. [A][B][C][D][E][F][G][H][I][J][K][L][M][N][O]   46. [A][B][C][D]
37. [A][B][C][D][E][F][G][H][I][J][K][L][M][N][O]   47. [A][B][C][D]
38. [A][B][C][D][E][F][G][H][I][J][K][L][M][N][O]   48. [A][B][C][D]

39. [A][B][C][D][E][F][G][H][I][J][K][L][M][N][O]   49. [A][B][C][D]
40. [A][B][C][D][E][F][G][H][I][J][K][L][M][N][O]   50. [A][B][C][D]

Part Four   Vocabulary

51. [A][B][C][D] 52. [A][B][C][D] 53. [A][B][C][D] 54. [A][B][C][D]
55. [A][B][C][D] 56. [A][B][C][D] 57. [A][B][C][D] 58. [A][B][C][D]
59. [A][B][C][D] 60. [A][B][C][D] 61. [A][B][C][D] 62. [A][B][C][D]
63. [A][B][C][D] 64. [A][B][C][D] 65. [A][B][C][D] 66. [A][B][C][D]
67. [A][B][C][D] 68. [A][B][C][D] 69. [A][B][C][D] 70. [A][B][C][D]

Part Five   Short Answer Questions

71. A proper topic for this passage may be _____ .

72. Men suffer more from air pollution because they _____.

73. What makes men's walking different from women's? _____ .

74. As far as body structures are concerned, _____ face more danger in climbing mountains.

75. How many differences between men and women are mentioned in this passage? _____.

Part Six   Translation

76. _____
77. _____
78. _____
79. _____
80. _____

Model Test 5

Part One   Writing

Directions: *For this part, you are allowed thirty minutes to write a composition on the topic* **The way to success**. *You should write at least 100 words, and base your composition on the outline (given in Chinese) below:*

1. 每个人都试图在事业上获得成功；
2. 获得成功的要素；
3. 我坚信……

Part Two   Listening Comprehension

Section A

Directions: *In this section you will hear 10 short conversations. At the end of each conversation, a question will be asked about what was said, both the conversation and the question will be spoken only once. After each question there will be a pause. During the pause, you must read the four choices marked A, B, C and D, and decide which is the best answer. Then mark the corresponding letter on the Answer sheet with a single line through the center.*

1. A. In a railway station.

   B. In a bus terminal.

   C. In a hotel room.

   D. In a restaurant.

2. A. Tom applied for a job.

   B. Tom was preferred to others.

   C. Tom wanted other jobs.

62

D. Tom was too unlucky.

3. A. The man can't tolerate any noise.

   B. The man is looking for an apartment.

   C. The man has missed his appointment.

   D. The woman is going to take train trip.

4. A. He has a strange personality.

   B. He's got emotion. al problems.

   C. His illness is beyond cure.

   D. His behavior is hard to explain.

5. A. It has just begun snowing.

   B. She doesn't like snowy days.

   C. It has been snowing for some time.

   D. She doesn't think it's going to snow.

6. A. Servant and hostess.

   B. Waiter and customer.

   C. Doorkeeper and visitor.

   D. Shop assistant and old customer.

7. A. One.

   B. Two.

   C. Three.

   D. Four.

8. A. Preparing for bed.

   B. Walking toward the campus.

   C. Looking for a place to live.

   D. Inviting some friends to visit.

9. A. The man lost his new camera at the airport.

   B. The man left his new camera in his friend's car.

   C. The man enjoyed using his new camera on his trip.

   D. The woman lost her new camera on her way to the airport.

10. A. He is sure the new chef is better.

    B. He wonders whether the new chef is an improvement.

    C. He hopes the new chef will stay longer than the old one did.

    D. He's going to see the new chef tonight.

Section B

Directions: *In this section, you will hear three short passages. At the end of each passage, you will hear some questions. Both the passage and the questions will be spoken only once. After you hear a question, you must choose the best answer from the four choices marked A, B, C and D, and decide which is the best answer. Then mark the corresponding letter on the Answer Sheet with a single line through the center.*

Passage 1

Questions 11 to 13 are based on the passage you have just heard.

11. A. Nobody came to talk to him.

    B. People didn't listen to him attentively.

    C. People kept interrupting him.

    D. People made fun of him.

12. A. Because people are passive listeners.

    B. Because people are unwilling to talk.

    C. Because people enjoy answering any question.

    D. Because people like to talk to you about themselves.

13. A. Be an attentive listener.

    B. Don't talk about yourselves.

    C. Be interested in yourselves.

    D. Talk less and do more.

Passage 2

Questions 14 to 16 are based on the passage you have just heard.

14. A. With the help of an old lady.

    B. Through the carelessness of their keeper.

    C. By pretending to be asleep.

    D. By an accident that broke open their cage.

15. A. To the nearby grassland.

    B. To the trainer's house.

    C. To an elderly lady's house.

D. To a nearby zoo.

16. A. Because she liked lions.

   B. Because she was fearless.

   C. Because the trainer told her not to be afraid.

   D. Because she mistook the lion for a big dog.

Passage 3

Question 17 to 20 are based on the passage you just heard.

17. A. Original paintings.

   B. Art books.

   C. Reproduction of famous paintings.

   D. Handicrafts.

18. A. A method of making toys.

   B. A new library system for children.

   C. A method of selling toys.

   D. A new library system for adults.

19. A. A toy library.

   B. A science library.

   C. An art library.

   D. A record library.

20. A. Books to read.

   B. Paintings.

   C. A place to receive education.

   D. A place to meet and play with other children.

Section C

Directions: *In this section, you will hear a passage of about 150 words three times. The passage is printed on your Answer Sheet with about 20 words missing. First you will hear the whole passage from the beginning to the end just to get a general idea of it. Then, in the second reading, you will hear a signal indicating the beginning of a pause after each sentence, sometimes two sentences or just part of a sentence. During the pause, you must write down the missing words you have just heard in the corresponding space on the An-*

A passage with 20 missing words

Doctors __(21)__ that about 40% of women over thirty in Britain are __(22)__. This __(23)__ may be __(24)__ as a large number of overweight people never __(25)__ medical advice. Many women are very __(26)__ about being overweight. They feel that it shows a __(27)__ of will-power or __(28)__ on their part. In __(29)__, fat women do not conform to the modern __(30)__ of beauty exemplified by __(31)__ models and young film stars who are __(32)__ thin. __(33)__ from aesthetic reasons, there are strong medical grounds for not overeating. Overweight people are particularly more __(34)__ to get heart disease and are easily tired by physical __(35)__. Losing weight would certainly make them feel __(36)__ and increase their life expectancy.

Some women feel __(37)__ about being fat and their guilt is expressed by eating more. It is a vicious circle. On the other hand, there are women who unnecessarily lose weight in order to conform to a model of social acceptability. Some of them end up __(38)__ themselves to death! So perhaps it might be better to try to __(39)__ fat people's __(40)__ than to try to re move the fat.

Part Three   Reading Comprehension

Section A

Directions: *In this section, there is a passage with 10 blanks. You are required to select one word for each blank from a list of choices given in a word bank following the passage. Read the passage through carefully before making your choices. Each choice in the bank is identified by a letter. Please mark the corresponding letter for each item on Answer Sheet with a single line through the center.* **You may not use any of words in the bank more than once.**

A passage with 10 blanks

Obesity (肥胖) has become an epidemic. Not only does obesity have more __(41)__ health consequences than smoking, drinking, or poverty, it also affects more people.

(42) 23 percent of Americans are obese. An additional 36 percent are overweight. By contrast, only 6 percent are heavy drinkers, 19 percent are daily smokers and 14 percent live in poverty.

Obesity rates are increasing   (43) . These rates used to be fairly stable: between 1960 and 1980, there was only a minor increase in the number of Americans who were overweight or obese. Since 1980, however, not only has the percentage increased, but much of the increase is   (44) in the "obese" category, which grew by 60 percent between 1991 and 2000. Because this increase is relatively   (45) , its full impact is still not known. Some   (46) conditions take years to develop. Current research may, if anything, understate the public health consequences of obesity.

The past 20 years have witnessed a significant   (47) change: Americans are exercising less while maintaining at least the same caloric intake. Desk jobs, an increase in the number of hours devoted to television watching, and car-friendly urban environments are some of the environmental changes that have combined to   (48) physical activity.

These changes affect other   (49) countries, too. For example, over the past 20 years, Great Britain and Germany have experienced obesity growth rates similar to those in the United States. But because they started from lower levels, obesity in those countries has not yet become an epidemic-level   (50) to public health.

Word Bank

A. concentrated	E. negative	I. facilitate	M. acute
B. recent	F. gradually	J. approximately	N. discourage
C. positive	G. Chronic	K. industrialized	O. dramatically
D. lifestyle	H. injury	L. threat	

Section B

Directions: *There are 2 passages in this section. Each passage is followed by some questions or unfinished statements. For each of them there are four choices marked A, B, C and D. You should decide on the best choice and mark the corresponding letter on Answer Sheet with a single line through th0e center.*

Passage 1

Questions 51 to 55 are based on the following passage.

By suing (起诉) Morris and Steel, McDonald's effectively forced the pair to prove conclusively that their criticisms of McDonald's published nearly a decade earlier were in fact all true, an apparently overwhelming legal task. Their condemnations are so numerous and so wide-ranging that the fields of inquiry are almost limitless, but Morris and Steel have surprised everyone with the tenacity of their defense.

The provocative six-page leaflet at the heart of the trial, "What's wrong with McDonald's?", was published in 1985 by the independent environmental pressure group Greenpeace London (not related to Greenpeace International). It accused McDonald's — under headings like McDollar, McGreedy, McCancer, McMurder, McRipoff and McGarbage — of torturing animals, manipulating children, underpaying its staff, exploiting the developing world, destroying rain forests and selling food which damages its customers' health.

A total of 27 pre-trial hearings and various appeals over the next few years delayed the trial, giving Steel and Morris time to prepare. They started by mastering court procedure, learning legal jargon (行话) and researching a wide range of scientific and technical details.

Over the years of the trial, the unemployed environmentalists have spent most of their waking hours mounting their dogged defense. Though the case was considered too complex for a jury, every point has been thoroughly argued and rebutted (驳斥) by the tenacious pair.

However, McDonald's remains equally determined to clear its name, and more than a decade after the company first took action, the case has cost it at least a million pounds — maybe as much as two million, according to some British press estimates.

Yet in mid-1996, for all its efforts, the company was still a long way from getting the result it wants. It has been a laborious process calling the 180 witnesses, most from outside Britain, to give their evidence in court. Morris claimed to have amassed more than 40,000 documents ready to produce as evidence for the pair's defense, and racks of files lined the courtroom shelves. Each day in court has produced another 80 pages of transcript.

Bankruptcy for Morris and Steel would inevitably follow any significant award of compensatory damages in favor of McDonald's but, ironically, it is their financial weakness that has made Morris and Steel such formidable (可怕的) and expensive opponents. Without mortgages or careers, they have little to lose. As Morris said recently, "Another 100 or even 200 days — it doesn't worry us".

"It's important to fight against these attempts by multinationals to silence criticism, but it's really exhausting and sometimes I wish I could have my life back," Steel admitted recently.

But the stakes are perhaps higher still for McDonald's. The company spent around 33.7 million pounds on advertising and promotion in the UK alone in 1992. Good public relations are crucial to its profitability, but its attempts to clear its name in this case have attracted a great deal more unfavorable publicity.

51. The word "tenacity" in the first paragraph most probably means _____ .

A. firmness

B. weakness

C. hardship

D. force

52. Morris and Steel was sued by McDonald's because _____.

A. they had joined an environmental pressure group

B. they had been stealing money for the company

C. they had destroyed forests and manipulated children

D. they had publish a pamphlet with merciless criticism of McDonald's

53. In spite of McDonald's huge expenditures and efforts in clearing its name,

_____.

A. McDonald's is sure to win the case very soon

B. Morris and Steel seem to be getting the upper hand

C. the case has in a way damaged its public relations

D. McDonald's will surely lose the case very soon

54. Morris and Steel's financial weakness _____.

A. has prevented them from producing enough evidence in court

B. has only made them strengthened in their resolve to prove their criticisms all true

C. has nearly frightened them into taking back what they had said about McDonald's

D. has worried them very much and greatly weakened the force of the defense

55. Which of the following is NOT TRUE about the trial according to the passage?

A. It has been a long, laborious and complicated process.

B. It has forced Morris and Steel to learn lots of things to conduct their own defense.

C. The publicity of the case has potential to increase McDonald's profits in Britain.

D. Both parties have made huge efforts and spent enormous amount of time, determined to win.

Passage 2

Questions 56 to 60 are based on the following passage.

Once upon a time, the United States seemed to have plenty of land to go around: plenty of rivers to dam and plenty of rural valleys left over; plenty of space for parks and factories and plenty of forests to cut and grasslands to plow. But that was once upon a time. The days of unused land are over. Now the land has been spoken for, fenced off, carved up into cities and farms and industrial parks, and put to use.

At the same time, the population keeps growing. People need places to work and places to play. So we need more sites for more industries, more beaches for more sunbathers and more clean rivers for more fishers. And it isn't just a matter of population growth. Our modern technology has needs that must be met, too. We need more coal for energy, and we need more power plants; cars must have highways and parking lots, and jets must have airports.

Each of these land uses swallows up precious space. Highways and expressways alone take some 200,000 acres each year. And urban sprawl — the spreading out of cities — is expected to gobble up vast areas of land by the year 2,000. But there is only so much land to go around. It is always hard to decide. Take, for example, a forest. A forest can be a timber supply. It can provide a home for wildlife. It is scenery and a recreation area for man. It is soil and watershed protection.

56. "... the United States seemed to have plenty of land to go around" means that
_____.

A. the United States seemed to have vast land for its people to walk around

B. the United States seemed to have enough land for sharing with everyone

C. the United States could provide whatever its inhabitants need

D. the United States was not able to allow its people to do what they wanted to

57. The sentence of "plenty of rivers to dam and plenty of rural valleys left over" suggests that _____.

A. the United States had a lot of rivers to dam and many rural valleys, too

B. the rivers could be dammed later

C. rural valleys would be considered in the future

D. people needn't think of the rivers and valleys

58. "Now the land has been spoken for ... " tells us that _____.

A. today, land has shown its values

B. now, people have said something about land

C. nowadays, land has been claimed by human beings

D. recently, people spoke for the land

59. The phrase of "swallows up" informed us that _____.

A. these uses of land have good results

B. these lands must be used totally

C. the precious space was taken completely

D. the precious space was eaten up

60. The word "sprawl" indicates that _____.

A. cities are developing very fast to meet the people's demands

B. urban areas are diminishing gradually

C. urban areas are enlarging steadily in a planned way

D. cities are spreading out without any plans

Part Four   Vocabulary

Directions: *Fou this part you are required to choose the best answer from A, B, C and D*
to complete the following sentences.

61. In our highly technological society, the number of job for unskilled workers is

_____.

A. shrinking   B. obscuring   C. altering   D. constraining

62. Generous public funding of basic science would _____ considerable benefits for the

country's health, wealth and security.

A. lead to   B. result from   C. lie in   D. settle down

63. Everybody _____ in the hall where they were welcomed by the secretary.

A. assembled   B. accumulated   C. piled   D. joined

64. The tomato juice left brown _____ on the front of my jacket.

A. pot   B. point   C. track   D. trace

65. I didn't _____ to take a taxi but I had to as I was late.

A. assume   B. suppose   C. mean   D. hope

66. I'm very sorry to have _____ you with so many questions on such an occasion.

    A. offended   B. impressed   C. bothered   D. interfered

67. Everything we eat and drink contains some salt; we can meet the body's need for it from natural sources without turning _____ the salt bottle.

    A. up   B. to   C. on   D. over

68. This book is expected to _____ the best-seller lists.

    A. exemplify   B. promote   C. prevail   D. dominate

69. A completely new situation will _____ when the examination system comes into existence.

    A. rose   B. rise   C. raise   D. arise

70. The manager spoke highly of such _____ as loyalty, courage and truthfulness shown by his employees.

    A. virtues   B. features   C. properties   D. characteristics

71. The old building is in a good state of _____ except for the wooden floors.

    A. observation   B. preservation   C. conservation   D. compensation

72. It is through learning that individual _____ many habitual ways of reacting to situations.

    A. retains   B. gains   C. achieves   D. acquires

73. I didn't _____ to take a taxi but I had to as I was late.

    A. assume   B. suppose   C. mean   D. hope

74. I think that I committed a _____ in asking her because she seemed very upset by my question.

    A. blunder   B. revenge   C. reproach   D. scandal

75. Ever since the rise of industrialism, education has been _____ towards producing workers.

    A. harnessed   B. hatched   C. motivated   D. geared

76. Our new house is very _____ for me as I can get to the office in five minutes.

    A. adaptable   B. comfortable   C. convenient   D. available

77. Among all the changes resulting from the _____ entry of women into the work force, the transformation that has occurred in the women themselves is not the least important.

    A. surplus   B. massive   C. quantitative   D. formidable

78. Tony is very disappointed _____ the results of the exam.

A. for   B. toward   C. on   D. with

79. Improved consumer confidence is _____ to an economic recovery.

    A. subordinate   B. cumulative   C. crucial   D. satisfactory

80. When business is _____ , there is usually an obvious increase in unemployment.

    A. degraded   B. depressed   C. reduced   D. lessened

Part Five   Short Answer Questions

Directions: *In this part there is a short passage with five questions or incomplete statements. Read the passage carefully. Then answer the questions or complete the statement in the fewest possible words.*

Questions 81 to 85 are based on the passage.

Many parents who welcome the idea of turning off the TV and spending more time with the family are still worried that without TV they would constantly be on call as entertainers for their children. They remember thinking up all sorts of things to do when they were kids. But their own kids seem different, less resourceful, somehow. When there's nothing to do, these parents observe regretfully, their kids seem unable to come up with any thing to do besides turning on the TV.

One father, for example, says, "When I was a kid, we were always thinking up things to do, projects and games. We certainly never complained in an annoying way to our parents", "I have nothing to do!" He compares this with his own children today: "They're simply lazy. If someone doesn't entertain them, they'll happily sit there watching TV all day. "

"There is one word for this father's disappointment: unfair. It is as if he were disappointed in them for not reading Greek though they have never studied the language. He deplores(哀叹) his children's lack of inventiveness, as if the ability to play were something innate(天生的) that his children are missing. In fact, while the tendency to play is built into the human species, the actual ability to play — to imagine, to invent, to elaborate on reality in a playful way — and the ability to gain fulfillment from it, these are skills that have to be learned and developed.

Such disappointment, however, is not only unjust, it is also destructive. Sensing their parents' disappointment, children come to believe that they are, indeed, lacking something, and that this makes them less worthy of admiration and respect. Giving children the opportunity to develop new resources, to enlarge their horizons and discover the pleasures of doing things on their own is, on the other hand, a way to help children develop a confident feeling about themselves as capable and interesting people.

81. According to many parents, without TV, their children would like them to _____.

82. Many parents think that, instead of watching a lot of TV, their children should _____.

83. The father often blames his children for not being able to entertain themselves. This is unfair because they _____.

84. When parents show constant disappointment in their children, the destructive effect is that the children will _____.

85. Developing children's self-confidence helps bring them up to be _____.

Part Six   Translation

Direcions: *Finish the sentences on Answer Sheet by translating into English.*

86. _____ (从他的口音判断), he must be a northerner.

87. The doctor advised that _____ (她应该节食) in order not to put on weight.

88. I didn't expect so heavy traffic, otherwise _____ (我就会早点动身).

89. When I arrived home, I found _____ (房子被破门而入了).

90. Jack was caught _____ (考试作弊).

Answer Sheet

Part One   Writing

The way to success

_____

_____

_____

_____

_____

_____

_____

_____

_____

_____

_____

_____

_____

_____

_____

_____

_____

_____

_____

_____

_____

_____

Part Two   Listening Comprehension

Section A

1. [A][B][C][D]   2. [A][B][C][D]   3. [A][B][C][D]   4. [A][B][C][D]
5. [A][B][C][D]   6. [A][B][C][D]   7. [A][B][C][D]   8. [A][B][C][D]
9. [A][B][C][D]   10. [A][B][C][D]

Section B

11. [A][B][C][D] 12. [A][B][C][D]   13. [A][B][C][D]   14. [A][B][C][D]
15. [A][B][C][D] 16. [A][B][C][D]   17. [A][B][C][D]   18. [A][B][C][D]
19. [A][B][C][D] 20. [A][B][C][D]

Section C

21. _____   22. _____   23. _____   24. _____   25. _____
26. _____   27. _____   28. _____   29. _____   30. _____
31. _____   32. _____   33. _____   34. _____   35. _____
36. _____   37. _____   38. _____   39. _____   40. _____

Part Three   Reading Comprehension

Section A

41. [A][B][C][D][E][F][G][H][I][J][K][L][M][N][O]
42. [A][B][C][D][E][F][G][H][I][J][K][L][M][N][O]
43. [A][B][C][D][E][F][G][H][I][J][K][L][M][N][O]
44. [A][B][C][D][E][F][G][H][I][J][K][L][M][N][O]
45. [A][B][C][D][E][F][G][H][I][J][K][L][M][N][O]
46. [A][B][C][D][E][F][G][H][I][J][K][L][M][N][O]
47. [A][B][C][D][E][F][G][H][I][J][K][L][M][N][O]
48. [A][B][C][D][E][F][G][H][I][J][K][L][M][N][O]
49. [A][B][C][D][E][F][G][H][I][J][K][L][M][N][O]
50. [A][B][C][D][E][F][G][H][I][J][K][L][M][N][O]

Section B

51. [A][B][C][D]
52. [A][B][C][D]
53. [A][B][C][D]
54. [A][B][C][D]
55. [A][B][C][D]
56. [A][B][C][D]
57. [A][B][C][D]
58. [A][B][C][D]
59. [A][B][C][D]
60. [A][B][C][D]

Part Four   Vocabulary

61. [A][B][C][D] 62. [A][B][C][D]   63. [A][B][C][D]   64. [A][B][C][D]

65. [A][B][C][D] 66. [A][B][C][D] 67. [A][B][C][D] 68. [A][B][C][D]

69. [A][B][C][D] 70. [A][B][C][D] 71. [A][B][C][D] 72. [A][B][C][D]

73. [A][B][C][D] 74. [A][B][C][D] 75. [A][B][C][D] 76. [A][B][C][D]

77. [A][B][C][D] 78. [A][B][C][D] 79. [A][B][C][D] 80. [A][B][C][D]

71. [A][B][C][D] 72. [A][B][C][D] 73. [A][B][C][D] 74. [A][B][C][D]

75. [A][B][C][D] 76. [A][B][C][D] 77. [A][B][C][D] 78. [A][B][C][D]

79. [A][B][C][D] 80. [A][B][C][D]

Part Five Short Answer Questions

81. According to many parents, without TV, their children would like them to _____ .

82. Many parents think that, instead of watching a lot of TV, their children should _____ .

83. The father often blames his children for not being able to entertain themselves. This is unfair because they _____ .

84. When parents show constant disappointment in their children, the destructive effect is that the children will _____ .

85. Developing children's self-confidence helps bring them up to be _____ .

Part Six Translation

86. _____

87. _____

88. _____

89. _____

90. _____

Model Test 6

Part One   Writing

Directions: *For this part, you are allowed thirty minutes to write a composition on the topic **A Letter of Application**. You should write at least 100 words, and base your composition on the outline (given in Chinese) below:*

有一国外学校欲在国内选若干名大学生去国外进修,请进行自我推荐并说明选择上该校的理由。

Part Two   Listening Comprehension

Section A

Directions: *In this section you will hear 10 short conversations. At the end of each conversation, a question will be asked about what was said, both the conversation and the question will be spoken only once. After each question there will be a pause. During the pause, you must read the four choices marked A, B, C and D, and decide which is the best answer. Then mark the corresponding letter on the Answer sheet with a single line through the center.*

1. A. At 10.

   B. At 10:30.

   C. At 11.

   D. At 11:30.

2. A. In the kitchen of a restaurant.

   B. In the office of a restaurant.

   C. On the telephone.

   D. In New York.

3. A. He does not like it at all.

   B. He prefers classical music to jazz.

78

C. He likes jazz more than classical music.

D. He likes jazz as much as classical music.

4. A. They weren't washed yet.

B. They weren't picked up by their owner.

C. They were not sent to the laundry.

D. They were dirty.

5. A. Classmates.

B. Teacher and student.

C. Shop assistant and customer.

D. Husband and wife.

6. A. It is wonderful.

B. It is not well-made.

C. It is out of fashion.

D. It is unfit.

7. A. She found the assignment very difficult.

B. The assignment was difficult to complete in 20 minutes.

C. She finds it hard to believe the man spent so long a time.

D. The man couldn't finish the assignment because he had other work to do.

8. A. Bob is good at running.

B. Bob works as a guard.

C. Bob never skips the professor's class.

D. Bob is very smart.

9. A. The woman will go walking with her friend.

B. The woman will rest and take care of herself.

C. The woman will stay at home and do her exercises.

D. The woman will catch up with her reading.

10. A. He is a short man.

B. He often complains.

C. He is a happy sort of person.

D. He is worried about something.

Section B

Directions: *In this section, you will hear three short passages. At the end of each pas-*

sage, you will hear some questions. Both the passage and the questions will be spoken only once. After you hear a question, you must choose the best answer from the four choices marked A, B, C and D, and decide which is the best answer. Then mark the corresponding letter on the Answer Sheet with a single line through the center.

Passage 1

Questions 11 to 13 are based on the passage you have just heard.

11. A. About 4,500.

    B. About 4,000.

    C. About 3,500.

    D. About 3,000.

12. A. It is the largest language family.

    B. It was originated 4,900 years ago.

    C. It contains all the languages spoken in Europe.

    D. Many of the present-day European and Indian languages are modern forms of it.

13. A. People's interest in how languages began.

    B. Languages today and past.

    C. The important language families.

    D. The English language in constant change.

Passage 2

Questions 14 to 16 are based on the passage you have just heard.

14. A. Marriage that continues for many years without divorce.

    B. Marriage that can easily end in divorce.

    C. People will marry three or four times in one lifetime.

    D. Divorced people don't stay single.

15. A. In modern society, people's lives don't stay the same for very long.

    B. They are not consistent.

    C. Americans like to change partners.

    D. They don't take marriage seriously.

16. A. Marriage is not popular in America because of too many divorces.

    B. Eighty percent of divorced people will still remarry in America.

C. In the new century, most American people will marry two or three times in one lifetime.

D. Americans frequently change their jobs and the places of living.

Passage 3

Question 17 to 20 are based on the passage you have just heard.

17. A. Your eye sight.

    B. Your driving ability.

    C. Your car's mechanical condition.

    D. Your knowledge of traffic regulations.

18. A. To practise driving with an experienced driver.

    B. To drive under normal highway condition.

    C. To have the car checked by the license officer.

    D. To us it as an identification card.

19. A. The license office provides the test vehicle.

    B. The examiner shows how to start, stop or park.

    C. The examiner watches you driving in your car.

    D. The test is carried out where there is little traffic.

20. A. Two.

    B. Three.

    C. Four.

    D. Five.

Section C

Directions: *In this section, you will hear a passage of about 150 words three times. The passage is printed on your Answer Sheet with about 20 words missing. First you will hear the whole passage from the beginning to the end just to get a general idea of it. Then, in the second reading, you will hear a signal indicating the beginning of u pause after each sentence, sometimes two sentences or just part of a sentence. During the pause, you must write down the missing words you have just heard in the corresponding space on the Answer Sheet. There is also a different signal indicating the end of the pause. When you hear this signal, you must get ready for what comes next from* *the recording. You can check what you have written when the passage is read to you once again without the pauses.*

A passage with 20 missing words

Life was __(21)__ __(22)__ for most people in London 100 years ago. They had to put up with noise, smoke and __(23)__ . The noise came from the __(24)__ , and the smoke and dirt came from the trains and the thousands of __(25)__ all around them. The smoke often mixed with __(26)__ and hung in the air for days. __(27)__ killed thousands of children. Families were large but often five out of seven children would die before they were five years old.

Is life really better than it was 100 years ago? It is certainly true that people live longer than they __(28)__ to, __(29)__ faster than they could and __(30)__ more things than they did. But we still have to put up with noise, __(31)__ and bad air. They are still a basic part of __(32)__ life.

100 years ago there was a (33) difference between town and country. But the __(34)__ car has changed all that. One __(35)__ can take up a huge __(36)__ of land. Cars are also a basic part of modern life.

But __(37)__ and modern life do not have to be __(38)__ of beauty. We can have both beauty and __(39)__ . We need clean rivers and open __(40)__ just as much as people did 100 years ago. But it's becoming more and more difficult to have open land, clear water and open air.

Part Three Reading Comprehension

Directions: *In this section, there is a passage with 10 blanks. You are required to select one word for each blank from a list of choices given in a word bank following the passage. Read the passage through carefully before making your choices. Each choice in the bank is identified by a letter. Please mark the corresponding letter for each item on Answer Sheet with a single line through the center.* ***You may not use any of words in the bank more than once.***

A passage with 10 blanks

There have been increasing news reports of incidents of harassment and violence directed at persons perceived to be Arab Americans or of Middle Eastern, including children. Arab-American parents have publicly expressed fear about the __(41)__ of their children at school. These occurrences are of __(42)__ concern to the Department of Education.

All of us are justly __(43)__ at the destruction and loss of life in New York, Washington, and Pennsylvania. However, violence and harassment against __(44)__ people based solely on their race or national origin only compounds hatred and must not be tolerated. Each incident has a ripple effect in our schools and our communities, creating fear and tensions that __(45)__ affect us all. I am concerned that young people are particularly __(46)__ to copying inappropriate conduct at a time when fear and anger are heightened .

Harassment in schools can take many forms, from __(47)__ name calling to violent crimes directed at a student because of his or her race, the country of origin of the student's family, or the student's cultural traditions. We are all __(48)__ to making sure children across America can attend school in a safe and secure environment __(49)__ from physical threats and discrimination. School officials, working closely with students, parents, and community groups play a critical role in __(50)__ that race-based harassment and violence have no place in our schools.

A. ultimately	E. healthy	I. free	M. various
B. primary	F. indifferent	J. automatically	N. safety
C. poverty	G. ensuring	K. abusive	O. innocent
D. inclined	H. committed	L. angry	

Section B

Directions: *There are 2 passages in this section. Each passage is followed by some questions or unfinished statements. For each of them there are four choices marked A, B, C and D. You should decide on the best choice and mark the corresponding letter on Answer Sheet with a single line through the center.*

Passage 1

Questions 51 to 55 are based on the following passage.

That is one way of arranging the survival game. The other extreme way of fixing the result is to have the right answers to all potentially disastrous experiments fitted in at the outset. Some animals are indeed built like this: sea anemones (海葵), for example. Any sea anemone knows what is edible and what is not. It will grasp food with its tentacles and cram it into the mouth. It will reject inedible objects and close up when poked. A sea anemone does not learn to do these things. They are property of the construction of its nervous system.

The fact that animals behave sensibly can be attributed partly to what we might call "genetic learning", to distinguish it from the individual learning that an animal does in the course of its own lifetime. Genetic learning is learned by a species as a whole, and it is achieved by selection of those members of each generation that happen to behave in the right way. However, genetic learning depends upon a prediction that the future will more or less exactly resemble the past. The more variable individual experience is likely to be, the less efficient is genetic learning as a means of getting over the problems of the survival game. And because most animals live in non-uniform environments, the details of which are liable to vary from one generation to the next, it is not surprising to find that very few species indeed depend wholly upon genetic learning. In the great majority of animals, behavior is a compound of individual experience superimposed upon an inherited bias to behave in a particular way.

51. What is most probably discussed in the part previous to this passage?

   A. Genetic learning.

   B. Individual learning /experience.

   C. Survival game/experiment.

   D. Nervous system.

52. What does the word "edible" in the first paragraph most probably mean?

   A. Due to be avoided.

   B. Pleasant to taste.

   C. Fit to be eaten.

   D. Dangerous to touch.

53. What is genetic learning according to the passage?

   A. The inherited knowledge of how to survive which an animal is born with.

   B. The knowledge of genetic selection which an animal pick up in its own lifetime.

   C. The answers to survival questions obtained in the course of the animal's adjustment to the environment.

   D. The experience picked up through trial and error in the game of survival.

54. The sea anemones can behave sensibly because _____.

A. they learn to do so after birth

B. the behavior is in-built in their genes

C. their parent tell them to do so

D. other animals teach them to do so

55. Because of the non-uniform environment, most animals _____ .

A. depend wholly on inherited bias of behavior

B. depend wholly on individual experience

C. learn to vary their behavioral patterns from time to time

D. combine individual experience with genetic learning

Passage Two

Questions 56 to 60 are based on the following passage.

The so-called Jungle of popular imagination, the tropical rain forest belt stretching around our planet at the Equator, has taken some 60 million years to evolve to its present state. It is quite simply the most complex, most important ecosystem on earth.

Homo habilis, Man the Builder, has tragically always seen the jungle as something alien, an environment to be vanquished or replaced with his own constructions. In the past twenty years the rate of pillage (掠夺) has increased alarmingly and huge tracts of verdant beautiful forest — an irreplaceable treasure house of living things — has given way often to wasteland. The evidence is that Man will redouble his destructive efforts until the forest 'system' is smashed, and the jungle will function no more.

Many experts gloomily predict that the tropical rain forests will finally vanish around the end of our century. Well done, 20th century!

What are the burning reasons that drive men to destroy our monumental inheritance?

Man seldom does anything for entirely rational reasons: usually, the less rational his 'reasons' are, the more he defends them with short-term economic arguments. That is one of the modern lessons in ecology.

"We need the land for people," runs the argument. Well, many people already inhabit the tropical forest belt. There, native tribes have their own low-impact life style, hunting, trapping and practicing a little cultivation. Perhaps not idyllic, it is nevertheless a life style that does not endanger the forest ecosystem.

56. The increased rate of pillage to the jungle may mean that _____ .

A. more and more jungle has been destroyed by men

B. an environment has vanished

C. the forest system is smashed and the jungle will not function any more

D. more woods were cut down

57. What does the writer mean by writing "Well done, 20th century!"?

A. It will be well-done in the 20th century.

B. It is the writer's irony to satire man's outstanding work — cutting down the jungle.

C. We will do better in the 21st century.

D. It is well-done for the forests to be vanished around the end of our century.

58. What is one of the modern lessons in ecology according to the passage?

A. Man does everything according to completely rational reason.

B. The more rational his reasons, the more he defends them with short-term economy.

C. Man often does something for irrational reasons.

D. The economic argument is the important reason.

59. More jungle is cultivated because _____.

A. it is the man's life style

B. people need more land to live

C. the old native tribes have their own low-impact life style

D. it will not do harm to the forest ecosystem

60. Which of the following statement is NOT true according to the passage?

A. The cultivation of the jungle has increased.

B. The jungle has existed on our planet for about 60 million years.

C. Man has rational reasons to cut down the trees.

D. Natives in the jungle have been living a low-impact life.

Part Four   Vocabulary

Directions: *For this part you are required to choose the best answer from A, B, C and D to complete the following sentences.*

61. Jobs and work do much more than most of us realize to provide happiness and

_____ .

  A. civilization   B. persistence   C. contentment   D. retirement

62. Work is _____ a necessary for most human beings; it is the focus of their life.

    A. more than   B. less than

    C. no more than   D. no less than

63. They stood gazing at the happy _____ of children playing in the park.

    A. perspective   B. view

    C. landscape   D. scene

64. Having finished their morning work, the clerks stood up behind their desks, _____ themselves.

    A. stretching   B. extending

    C. prolonging   D. expanding

65. No on can function properly if they are _____ of adequate sleep.

    A. deprived   B. ripped

    C. stripped   D. contrived

66. The prisoner was _____ of his civil liberty for three years.

    A. discharged   B. derived

    C. deprived   D. dispatched

67. To prevent flooding in winter the water flowing from the dam is constantly _____ by a computer.

    A. managed   B. monitored

    C. graded   D. conducted

68. My hands and feet were _____ with cold as I waited for the bus.

    A. cliff   B. still   C. stiff   D. stick

69. Without proper lessons, you could _____ a lot of bad habits when playing the piano.

    A. keep up   B. pick up   C. draw up   D. catch up

70. Some people think that a _____ translation, or word-for-word translation, is easier than a free translation.

    A. literal   B. literary   C. liberal   D. linear

71. The director gave me his _____ that he would double my pay if I did my job well.

    A. warrant   B. obligation   C. assurance   D. certainty

72. The basic causes are unknown, although certain conditions that may lead to cancer have been _____ .

    A. identified   B. guaranteed   C. notified   D. conveyed

73. _____ his loss of the Olympic gold medals and a sad decline in fortune during his later years, Thorpe was almost unanimously chosen the greatest athlete of modern times.

    A. Despite   B. In spite

    C. However   D. Although

74. Operations which left patients _____ and in need of long periods of recovery time now leave them feeling relaxed and comfortable.

    A. exhausted   B. abandoned   C. injured   D. deserted

75. They would start off by saying that "everyone know" the earth to be round, and if pressed _____, would become angry.

    A. to a greater extent B. more   C. further   D. again

76. Those gifts of rare books that were given to us were deeply _____.

    A. appealed   B. appreciated   C. applied   D. approved

77. It is difficult to _____ of a plan to end poverty.

    A. ponder   B. reckon   C. speculate   D. conceive

78. In Britain people _____ four million tons of potatoes every year.

    A. swallow   B. dispose   C. consume   D. exhaust

79. The price of beer _____ from 50 cents to $ 4 per liter during the summer season.

    A. ranged   B. differed   C. altered   D. separated

80. Even when textbooks are _____ through a school system, methods of teaching may vary greatly.

    A. commonplace   B. standardized

    C. competitive   D. generalized

Part Five   Short Answer Questions

Directions: *In this part there is a short passage with five questions or incomplete statements. Read the passage carefully. Then answer the questions or complete the statement in the fewest possible words.*

Questions 81 to 85 are based on the passage.

    Sports is one of the world's largest industries, and most athletes are professionals who are well paid for their efforts. Because an athlete succeeds by achievement only—not by economic background or family connections—sports can be a fast route to wealth, and many athletes play more for money than for love.

This has not always been true. In the ancient Olympics the winner got only a wreath of olive leaves (橄榄叶花环). Even though the winners became national heroes, the games remained amateur for centuries. Athletes won fame, but no money. As time passed, however, the contests became increasingly less amateur and cities began to hire athletes to represent them. By the fourth century A. D. , the Olympics were ruined, and they were soon ended.

In 1896，the Olympic games were revived (使再度兴起) with the same goal of pure amateur competition. The rules bar athletes who have ever received a ＄50 prize or an athletic scholarship, or who have spent four weeks in a training camp. At least one competitor in the 1896 games met all these qualifications. He was Spiridon Loues, a water carrier who won the marathon race. After the race, a rich Athenian offered him anything he wanted. A true amateur, Loues accepted only a cart and a horse. Then he gave up running forever. But Loues was an exception and now, as the Chairman of the German Olympic Committee said, "Nobody pays any attention to these rules." Many countries pay their athletes to train year-round, and Olympic athletes are eager to sell their names to companies that make everything from ski equipment to fast food.

Even the games themselves have become a huge business. Countries fight to hold the Olympics not only for honor, but for money. The 1972 games in Munich cost the Germans 545 million dollars, but by selling, TV rights, food, drink, hotel rooms, and souvenirs (纪念品), they managed to make a profit. Appropriately, the symbol of victory in the Olympic games is no longer a simple olive wreath—it is a gold medal.

81. To many people, sports today is nothing but _____.

82. What reward could an ancient Greek athlete expect?

83. By the fourth century A. D, Olympic contests became increasingly more _____, thus ruining the Olympics.

84. What did Spiridon Loues do after he accepted the Athenian's gift?

85. According to the author, some athletes are even willing to advertise for businesses which sell things like _____ .

Part Six　Translation

Directions: *Finish the sentences on Answer Sheet by translating into English*.

86. _____ (看在你哥哥的份上)，I can lend you my car to get around your transport problem.

87. He didn't pay his taxes and _____(结果以坐牢告终).

88. She makes jokes when she's disappointed, _____(而不是发脾气).

89. In the two world wars, tens of millions of people were _____(遭受了巨大的痛苦).

90. Don't _____(为这点小事大惊小怪的) because that is the last thing I expected.

Answer Sheet

Part One   Writing

A Letter of Application

Part Two　Listening Comprehension

Section A

1. [A][B][C][D]　2. [A][B][C][D]　3. [A][B][C][D]　4. [A][B][C][D]
5. [A][B][C][D]　6. [A][B][C][D]　7. [A][B][C][D]　8. [A][B][C][D]
9. [A][B][C][D]　10. [A][B][C][D]

Section B

11. [A][B][C][D] 12. [A][B][C][D]　13. [A][B][C][D]　14. [A][B][C][D]
15. [A][B][C][D] 16. [A][B][C][D]　17. [A][B][C][D]　18. [A][B][C][D]
19. [A][B][C][D] 20. [A][B][C][D]

Section C

21. _____　22. _____　23. _____　24. _____　25. _____
26. _____　27. _____　28. _____　29. _____　30. _____
31. _____　32. _____　33. _____　34. _____　35. _____
36. _____　37. _____　38. _____　39. _____　40. _____

Part Three　Reading Comprehension

Section A

41. [A][B][C][D][E][F][G][H][I][J][K][L][M][N][O]
42. [A][B][C][D][E][F][G][H][I][J][K][L][M][N][O]
43. [A][B][C][D][E][F][G][H][I][J][K][L][M][N][O]
44. [A][B][C][D][E][F][G][H][I][J][K][L][M][N][O]
45. [A][B][C][D][E][F][G][H][I][J][K][L][M][N][O]
46. [A][B][C][D][E][F][G][H][I][J][K][L][M][N][O]
47. [A][B][C][D][E][F][G][H][I][J][K][L][M][N][O]
48. [A][B][C][D][E][F][G][H][I][J][K][L][M][N][O]
49. [A][B][C][D][E][F][G][H][I][J][K][L][M][N][O]
50. [A][B][C][D][E][F][G][H][I][J][K][L][M][N][O]

Section B

51. [A][B][C][D]
52. [A][B][C][D]
53. [A][B][C][D]
54. [A][B][C][D]
55. [A][B][C][D]
56. [A][B][C][D]
57. [A][B][C][D]
58. [A][B][C][D]
59. [A][B][C][D]
60. [A][B][C][D]

Part Four　Vocabulary

61. [A][B][C][D] 62. [A][B][C][D]　63. [A][B][C][D]　64. [A][B][C][D]

65. [A][B][C][D] 66. [A][B][C][D] 67. [A][B][C][D] 68. [A][B][C][D]
69. [A][B][C][D] 70. [A][B][C][D] 71. [A][B][C][D] 72. [A][B][C][D]
73. [A][B][C][D] 74. [A][B][C][D] 75. [A][B][C][D] 76. [A][B][C][D]
77. [A][B][C][D] 78. [A][B][C][D] 79. [A][B][C][D] 80. [A][B][C][D]
71. [A][B][C][D] 72. [A][B][C][D] 73. [A][B][C][D] 74. [A][B][C][D]
75. [A][B][C][D] 76. [A][B][C][D] 77. [A][B][C][D] 78. [A][B][C][D]
79. [A][B][C][D] 80. [A][B][C][D]

Part Five　Short Answer Questions

81. To many people, sports today is nothing but _____.

82. What reward could an ancient Greek athlete expect?

83. By the fourth century A. D, Olympic contests became increasingly more _____, thus ruining the Olympics.

84. What did Spiridon Loues do after he accepted the Athenian's gift?

85. According to the author, some athletes are even willing to advertise for businesses which sell things like _____ .

Part Six　Translation

86. _____

87. _____

88. _____

89. _____

90. _____

Model Test 7

Part One   Writing

Directions: *For this part, you are allowed thirty minutes to write a composition on the topic **On Students Paying Back the Loan**. You should write at least 100 words, and base your composition on the outline (given in Chinese) below:*

1. 一些申请国家助学贷款的大学生不能按时还贷；
2. 产生这种现象的原因；
3. 我的看法。

Part Two   Listening Comprehension

Section A

Directions: *In this section you will hear 10 short conversations. At the end of each conversation, a question will be asked about what was said, both the conversation and the question will be spoken only once. After each question there will be a pause. During the pause, you must read the four choices marked A, B, C and D, and decide which is the best answer. Then mark the corresponding letter on the Answer sheet with a single line through the center.*

1. A. 6:15.
   B. 6:40.
   C. 5:35.
   D. 6:01.

2. A. They are going to their house which is air-conditioned.
   B. They are going to the cinema.
   C. They are going to buy an air-conditioner.

94

D. They are going to watch a play.

3. A. About 40.

   B. More than 40.

   C. Half of the student body.

   D. About 20.

4. A. A book seller.

   B. An operator.

   C. A pedestrian.

   D. A policewoman.

5. A. The woman should return later.

   B. The woman must complete paper work.

   C. The woman's application was lost in files.

   D. The woman is not suitable for the job.

6. A. It's a shame to be late.

   B. What a pity!

   C. I'm happy to hear that.

   D. No problem.

7. A. Because he has no experience.

   B. Because he has the experience to do it.

   C. Because he will do it better if he has experience.

   D. Because his experiment is not very difficult.

8. A. Modern poetry.

   B. Cumming's poetry.

   C. Traditional poetry.

   D. Beautiful poetry.

9. A. She thought they were expensive.

   B. She thought they were cheap.

   C. She liked the books.

   D. She didn't like the books.

10. A. It is too old.

    B. Some of the items cannot be moved out of it.

    C. She can't afford to buy a new one.

    D. Its size is adequate.

Section B

Directions: *In this section, you will hear three short passages. At the end of each passage, you will hear some questions. Both the passage and the questions will be spoken only once. After you hear a question, you must choose the best answer from the four choices marked A, B, C and D, and decide which is the best answer. Then mark the corresponding letter on the Answer Sheet with a single line through the center.*

Passage 1

Questions 11 to 13 are based on the passage you have just heard.

11. A. They have no other choice.

B. They think they can get the container free of charge.

C. The container is too attractive.

D. They believe the cost of the container is included in the cost of the product.

12. A. A buyer will not get what he wants to.

B. A buyer will gain more than he loses.

C. A buyer will get what he pays for.

D. A buyer will get something useful free of charge.

13. A. Do not buy the product which is sold in a glass or dish.

B. The best choice for a buyer is to get a product in a plain package.

C. The quality of a container has nothing to do with the quality of the product.

D. A buyer should get what he needs most.

Passage 2

Questions 14 to 16 are based on the passage you have just heard.

14. A. Grocery store.

B. Supermarket.

C. Fast-food restaurant.

D. Hotels and bars.

15. A. After they order their food, the customers usually wait just a few minutes.

B. The customers carry the food to a table themselves.

C. For many people the service at the fast-food restaurant is more important than the quality of food.

    D. Customers can't take the hamburgers away.

16. A. At the fast-food restaurant, the service is fast and the food is inexpensive.

    B. At the fast-food restaurant, the food has the best quality.

    C. The fast-food restaurants are more beautiful and cleaner than the ordinary oens.

    D. The fast-food restaurant provide different food.

Passage 3

Questions 17 to 20 are based on the passage you have just heard.

17. A. Dirty language that a program contains on TV.

    B. The amount of violence their children see on TV.

    C. Sexual content that a program contains on TV.

    D. Sexual images that can be easily found on computers.

18. A. At the beginning of and every now and then during the TV program.

    B. Only at the beginning of the TV program.

    C. From the beginning to the end of the TV program.

    D. Five minutes before the beginning of the TV program.

19. A. Being afraid of losing the race for president election.

    B. Being afraid of becoming public figures.

    C. Their behavior being criticized by politicians from both parties.

    D. Their personal privacy being revealed to the public.

20. A. Because he was disabled.

    B. Because he was weak.

    C. Because he was dishonest.

    D. Because he was too old.

Section C

Directions: *In this section, you will hear a passage of about 150 words three times. The passage is printed on your Answer Sheet with about 20 words missing. First you will hear the whole passage from the beginning to the end just to get a general idea of it. Then, in the second reading, you will hear a signal indicating the beginning of a pause after each sentence, sometimes two sentences or just part of a sentence. During the pause, you must write down*

the missing words you have just heard in the corresponding space on the An-
swer Sheet. There is also a different signal indicating the end of the pause.
When you hear this signal, you must get ready for what comes next from
the recording. You can check what you have written when the passage is
read to you once again without the pauses.

A passage with 20 missing words

Television now plays such an important part in many people's lives. It is ___(21)___
for us to try to decide whether it is a ___(22)___ or a curse. ___(23)___ television has both
advantages and disadvantages. But do the former outweigh the ___(24)___ ?

In the first place, television is not only a ___(25)___ source of ___(26)___ but also a
___(27)___ cheap one. People can just sit comfortably at home and enjoy an endless series
of programmes rather than go out in search of ___(28)___ elsewhere. Some people,
___(29)___ , maintain that this is precisely where the danger lies. The television viewer
need do nothing. He is completely ___(30)___ and has everything presented to him without
any effort on his part. Secondly, television keeps one ___(31)___ about current events, allows one to follow the ___(32)___ developments in science and politics. Yet here again
there is a danger. The television screen itself has a terrible, almost physical ___(33)___ for
us. We get so used to looking at its movements, so ___(34)___ on its pictures, that it begins to ___(35)___ our lives.

There are many other ___(36)___ for and against television. The poor quality of its
programmes is often ___(37)___ . But it is ___(38)___ a great comfort to many lonely elderly people. And does it corrupt or ___(39)___ our children? I think we must realize that
television in itself is neither good nor bad. It is the uses to which it is put that determine
its ___(40)___ to society.

Part Three   Reading Comprehension

Directions: *In this section, there is a passage with 10 blanks. You are required to select*
one word for each blank from a list of choices given in a word bank follow-
ing the passage. Read the passage through carefully before making your
choices. Each choice in the bank is identified by a letter. Please mark the
corresponding letter for each item on Answer Sheet with a single line
through the center. **You may not use any of words in the bank more than**

once .

A passage with 10 blanks

Asked to name their favorite city, many Americans would select San Francisco. San Francisco began as a __(41)__ Spanish outpost located on a magnificent bay. The town was little more than a village serving ranchers when the United States took __(42)__ of it in 1846 during the war with Mexico.

San Francisco __(43)__ into a city overnight because of the nearby discovery of gold in 1848. A great __(44)__ to California took place. Wagon trains plodded their __(45)__ way across 2,000 miles of prairie and mountains, while hundreds of sailing vessels made the __(46)__ hazardous trip around the Horn. The vessels disgorged (吐出) thousands of passengers, then the crews __(47)__ their ships and hundreds of vessels were left to rot in the bay. Within two years, California had enough population to become a __(48)__ and San Francisco was for many years the hub of that newly-arrived population.

The city's present __(49)__ is due to an excellent climate, an easy style of living, good food, and numerous tourist attractions. The city is famous for its cable cars which "clang and bang" up the __(50)__ hills, and for its excellent seafood stalls along the wharf. Most visitors arriving from nations in the Pacific Basin spend several days getting to know the town.

A. deserted	E. possession	I. seized	M. hopefully
B. popularity	F. sprang	J. equally	N. flat
C. shrank	G. pollution	K. steep	O. rush
D. small	H. dangerous	L. state	

Section B

Directions: *There are 2 passages in this section. Each passage is followed by some questions or unfinished statements. For each of them there are four choices marked A, B, C and D. You should decide on the best choice and mark the corresponding letter on Answer Sheet with a single line through the center.*

Passage 1

Questions 51 to 55 are based on the following passage.

Nearly 54 million cars and trucks in the United States are equipped with driver-side air bags located in the center of the steering wheel. 24 million also have a passenger-side device located in the dashboard. Air bags are designed to protect against sudden, fierce frontal highway impacts.

Five years ago evidence of serious air-bag injuries began to surface. Drivers in minor fender benders suffered severe eye and ear injuries, broken bones and third-degree burns from the force of the inflating bags.

In December 1991 the National Highway Traffic Safety Administration (NHTSA) advised parents to avoid putting rear-facing infant sets in front of air bags, acknowledging that the force of the explosive bag could harm infants, whose heads were only inches away from the devices.

Last October it was determined that all children of 12 and under were more susceptible to injury and death than adults; their more fragile bodies were seated lower, increasing the impact of the air bag to the head area. In addition, more children were not properly restrained or were out of position when the air bag inflated. On November 22, 1996, after nearly 60 deaths and thousands of injuries were attributed to the devices, the NHTSA mandated improved labels for all new vehicles, warning of the risk to children under 13. Despite these problems, officials stress the overall effectiveness of these devices. "All in all, air bags work well and are responsible for an 11 percent reduction in driver fatalities," says NHTSA Administrator Dr. Ricardo Martinez.

"First and foremost, make sure you're properly buckled up before getting on the road," says Brain O'Neill, president of the Insurance Institute for Highway Safety. Keep in mind how close you sit to an air bag. Push seats as far back as possible, remaining just close enough to control the pedals. Your face and torso should be at least ten to 12 inches from the steering column. "It's not a bad idea actually to measure the distance with a ruler to be sure," adds O'Neill.

Adjustable steering wheels should be pointed toward the chest rather than the head to prevent inflating bag from damaging the face or neck. Also, position hands at nine o'clock and three o'clock on the wheel to keep your arms away from an opening air bag.

Pregnant women in particular should keep their abdomen as distant from the air bag as possible. In the final trimester, women should point adjustable steering wheel upward, away from the fetus(胎儿).

Perhaps most important, children of 12 and under should always ride in the back seat, buckled up.

51. From the passage, we learned that _____ .

   A. there are 24 million cars and trucks in the United States

   B. there are 78 million car and trucks in the United States

   C. there are 24 million cars and trucks equipped with air-bags in the United States

   D. there are 78 million cars and trucks equipped with air-bags in the United States

52. The air bags are _____ .

   A. safe devices which can protect drivers from being hurt during highway accidents

   B. devices which are dangerous to small children

   C. safety devices which save 11% American drivers

   D. safety devices but need to be improved

53. The air-bag is located in the center of the steering wheel, so you should _____ .

   A. keep in mind how close you sit to an air bag

   B. push the front seat as far back as possible, remaining just close enough to control the pedal

   C. keep your face and torso at least 10 to 12 inches from the steering column

   D. do all the things mentioned the above

54. Adjustable steering wheels should _____ .

   A. be pointed toward the chest

   B. be pointed toward the abdomen

   C. be driven at 3 o'clock

   D. keep your arms away from an opening air bag

55. "The air bags are a good safety device, but children 12 and under should always ride in the back seat, buckled up" means _____ .

   A. air bags are no good for children

   B. air bags are only good for the parents who have more than 12 children

   C. children should sit in the back seat and wear safety belt though air bags are good life-saving devices

   D. the front seat is unsafe for young people

Passage 2

Questions 56 to 60 are based on the following passage.

   A scientist who does research in economic psychology and who wants to predict the way in which consumers will spend their money must study consumer behavior. He must obtain data both on resources of consumers and on the motives that tend to encourage or discourage money spending.

If an economist is asked which of three groups borrow most — people with rising incomes, stable incomes, or declining incomes — he would probably answer: those with declining incomes. Actually, in the years 1947 - 1950, the answer was: people with rising incomes. People with declining incomes were next and people with stable incomes borrowed the least. This shows us that traditional assumptions about earning and spending are not always reliable. Another traditional assumption is that if people who have money expect prices to go up, they will hasten to buy. If they expect prices to go down, they will postpone buying. But research surveys have shown that this is not always true. The expectations of price increase may not stimulate buying. One typical attitude was expressed by the wife of a mechanic in an interview at a time of rising prices. "In a few months," she said, "we'll have to pay more for meat and milk; we'll have less to spend on other things." Her family had been planning to buy a new car but they postponed this purchase. Furthermore, the rise in prices that has already taken place may be resented and buyer's resistance may be evoked.

The investigations mentioned above were carried out in America. Investigations conducted at the same time in Great Britain, however, yielded results that were more in agreement with traditional assumptions about saving and spending patterns. The condition most conducive to spending appears to be price stability. If prices have been stable and people consider that they are reasonable, they are likely to buy. Thus, it appears that the common business policy of maintaining stable prices is based on a correct understanding of consumer psychology.

56. If a scientist wants to study consumer behavior, what must he do?

    A. He must predict the way in which consumers will spend their money.

    B. He must do scientific research.

    C. He must know background of customers.

    D. He must collect information about the paying ability of customers and study their psychology.

57. Which of the following groups borrow money most according to traditional assumption?

    A. People who earn more and more.

B. People who have fixed incomes.

C. People who earn less and less.

D. None of the above.

58. Which of the following statements is NOT true according to the passage?

A. Traditional assumptions about earning and spending are not always reliable.

B. The condition that helps most in stimulating spending appears to be price rising.

C. Maintaining stable prices is a common business policy.

D. The results of the investigation in America were not the same as those in Great Britain.

59. The research survey in America has shown that when prices rise, _____.

A. people will hasten to buy

B. people will stop buying

C. people will postpone their purchase

D. people will buy more than they can use

60. The saving and spending patterns in America are _____ those at the same time in Britain.

A. different from

B. much better than

C. the same as

D. much worse than

Part Four   Vocabulary

Directions: *Fou this part you are required to choose the best answer from A , B , C and D to complete the following sentences.*

61. Our journey was slow because the train stopped _____ at different villages.

   A. unceasingly   B. gradually   C. continuously   D. continually

62. When there are small children around, it is necessary to put bottles of pills out of _____.

   A. distance   B. sight   C. reach   D. way

63. This crop does not do well in soils _____ the one for which it has been specially developed.

   A. outside   B. other than   C. beyond   D. rather than

64. The younger person's attraction to stereos cannot be explained only _____ famil-

iarity with technology.

    A. by means of B. in terms of   C. in quest of   D. by virtue of

65. The surface would have to be _____ from too frequent visiting.

    A. protected   B. prevented   C. derived   D. saved

66. Underground living may seem old and _____ at first thought.

    A. constant   B. hellish   C. palatable   D. repulsive

67. That night, we fell asleep with the _____ of Ten Sleep in our ears.

    A. wildlife   B. mess   C. roar   D. stock

68. In those days, the Indians _____ distances by the number of sleeps and the halfway mark between those two camps was exactly ten sleeps.

    A. weighed   B. measured   C. calculated   D. marked

69. The rough edges are _____ because people know they have to cooperate.

    A. worked off   B. worked up   C. worked away   D. worked out

70. Working for the best company in the community can provide employees with both _____ and self-confidence.

    A. state   B. stature   C. statue   D. status

71. Patient's bills of rights require that they _____ informed about their condition and about alternative for treatment.

    A. will be   B. are   C. have to be   D. be

72. Nurses may bitterly resent _____ take part, day after day, in deceiving patients, but feel powerless to take a stand.

    A. having to   B. to have to   C. having had to   D. they have to

73. Though many amateur athletes had played _____ pay _____ false names, Thorpe had used his own name.

    A. with...by   B. with...under   C. for... by   D. for...under

74. _____ his loss of the Olympic gold medals and a sad decline in fortune during his later years, Thorpe was almost unanimously chosen the greatest athlete of modern times.

    A. Despite   B. In spite   ·C. However   D. Although

75. My second card is the earth's shadow: when _____ on the moon during eclipses, it appears to be the shadow of a round object.

    A. reflected   B. flung   C. slung   D. cast

76. The answer is that I don't know, but have taken this piece of information _____

from newspaper articles and science booklets.

    A. accidentally   B. blindly   C. intentionally   D. on purpose

77. To _____ is to save and protect, to leave what we ourselves enjoy in such good condition that others may also share the enjoyment.

    A. converse   B. conceive   C. convert   D. contrive

78. In previous times, when fresh meat was in short _____, pigeons were kept by many households as a source of food.

    A. store   B. reserve   C. supply   D. provision

79. Some activist on the work force exclaimed that the workers had no business _____ $ 5 and a few competitive bonuses while the bosses collected hundreds of dollars each.

    A . conceding   B. compromising about C. settling for   D. agreeing with .

80. One Sunday morning my attention was _____ to the odd goings-on of our two youngest sons.

    A. delivered   B. diverted   C. absorbed   D. drawn

Part Five   Short Answer Questions

Directions: *In this part there is a short passage with five questions or incomplete state-ments. Read the passage carefully. Then answer the questions or complete the statement in the fewest possible words.*

Questions 81 to 85 are based on the passage.

    Earlier experiences influence subsequent behaviour is evidence of an obvious but nev-ertheless remarkable activity called remembering. Learning could not occur without the function popularly named memory. Constant practice has such an effect on memory as to lead to skillful performance on the piano, to recitation of a poem, and even to reading and understanding these words. So-called intelligent behaviour demands memory, remember-ing being a primary requirement for reasoning. The ability to solve any problem or even to recognize that a problem exists depends on memory. Typically, the decision to cross a street is based on remembering many earlier experiences.

    Practice (or review) tends to build and maintain memory for a task or for any learned material. Over a period of no practice what has been learned tends to be forgot-ten; and the adaptive consequences may not seem obvious. Yet, dramatic instances of sudden forgetting can be seen to be adaptive. In this sense, the ability to forget can be interpreted to have survived through a process of natural selection in animals. Indeed, when one's memory of an emotionally painful experience leads to serious anxiety, forgetting may produce relief. Nevertheless, an evolutionary interpretation might make it difficult to understand how the commonly gradual process of forgetting survived natural selection.

In thinking about the evolution of memory together with all its possible aspects, it is helpful to consider what would happen if memories failed to fade. Forgetting clearly aids orientation in time, since old memories weaken and the new tend to stand out, providing clues for inferring duration. Without forgetting, adaptive ability would suffer; for example, learned behaviour that might have been correct a decade ago may no longer be. Cases are recorded of people who (by ordinary standards) forgot so little that their everyday activities were full of confusion. Thus forgetting seems to serve the survival of the individual and the species.

Another line of thought assumes a memory storage system of limited capacity that provides adaptive flexibility specifically through forgetting. In this view, continual adjustments are made between learning or memory storage (input) and forgetting (output). Indeed, there is evidence that the rate at which individuals forget is directly related to how much they have learned. Such data offer gross support of contemporary models of memory that assume an input-output balance.

81. According to Para. 1, memory plays an important role in _____.

82. We can obviously notice that over a period of no practice what has been learned tends to be forgotten from _____.

83. It seems that the author disagree to explain _____.

84. If memories failed to fade, _____.

85. According to the assumption given in the last paragraph, we don't exactly know _____.

Part Six   Translation

Directions: *Finish the sentences on Answer Sheet by translating into English.*

86. He applied for a job only _____ (结果被拒绝).

87. The more I thought about it, _____ (我越觉得惭愧).

88. _____ (过分担心一次失败是没有用的), and we should draw some useful lessons from it.

89. Dick was sent to the hospital _____ (在交通事故中受了点轻伤).

90. In the past few years, perhaps no other topics _____ (更受年轻人关注了) than the bid for the sponsorship of the Olympic Games.

Answer Sheet

Part One   Writing

On Students Paying Back the Loan

_____

_____

_____

_____

_____

_____

_____

_____

_____

_____

_____

_____

_____

_____

_____

_____

_____

_____

_____

_____

Part Two Listening Comprehension

Section A

1. [A][B][C][D] 2. [A][B][C][D] 3. [A][B][C][D] 4. [A][B][C][D]
5. [A][B][C][D] 6. [A][B][C][D] 7. [A][B][C][D] 8. [A][B][C][D]
9. [A][B][C][D] 10. [A][B][C][D]

Section B

11. [A][B][C][D] 12. [A][B][C][D] 13. [A][B][C][D] 14. [A][B][C][D]
15. [A][B][C][D] 16. [A][B][C][D] 17. [A][B][C][D] 18. [A][B][C][D]
19. [A][B][C][D] 20. [A][B][C][D]

Section C

21. _____ 22. _____ 23. _____ 24. _____ 25. _____
26. _____ 27. _____ 28. _____ 29. _____ 30. _____
31. _____ 32. _____ 33. _____ 34. _____ 35. _____
36. _____ 37. _____ 38. _____ 39. _____ 40. _____

Part Three Reading Comprehension

Section A

41. [A][B][C][D][E][F][G][H][I][J][K][L][M][N][O]
42. [A][B][C][D][E][F][G][H][I][J][K][L][M][N][O]
43. [A][B][C][D][E][F][G][H][I][J][K][L][M][N][O]
44. [A][B][C][D][E][F][G][H][I][J][K][L][M][N][O]
45. [A][B][C][D][E][F][G][H][I][J][K][L][M][N][O]
46. [A][B][C][D][E][F][G][H][I][J][K][L][M][N][O]
47. [A][B][C][D][E][F][G][H][I][J][K][L][M][N][O]
48. [A][B][C][D][E][F][G][H][I][J][K][L][M][N][O]
49. [A][B][C][D][E][F][G][H][I][J][K][L][M][N][O]
50. [A][B][C][D][E][F][G][H][I][J][K][L][M][N][O]

Section B

51. [A][B][C][D]
52. [A][B][C][D]
53. [A][B][C][D]
54. [A][B][C][D]
55. [A][B][C][D]
56. [A][B][C][D]
57. [A][B][C][D]
58. [A][B][C][D]
59. [A][B][C][D]
60. [A][B][C][D]

Part Four   Vocabulary

61. [A][B][C][D] 62. [A][B][C][D]   63. [A][B][C][D]   64. [A][B][C][D]
65. [A][B][C][D] 66. [A][B][C][D]   67. [A][B][C][D]   68. [A][B][C][D]
69. [A][B][C][D] 70. [A][B][C][D]   71. [A][B][C][D]   72. [A][B][C][D]
73. [A][B][C][D] 74. [A][B][C][D]   75. [A][B][C][D]   76. [A][B][C][D]
77. [A][B][C][D] 78. [A][B][C][D]   79. [A][B][C][D]   80. [A][B][C][D]
71. [A][B][C][D] 72. [A][B][C][D]   73. [A][B][C][D]   74. [A][B][C][D]
75. [A][B][C][D] 76. [A][B][C][D]   77. [A][B][C][D]   78. [A][B][C][D]
79. [A][B][C][D] 80. [A][B][C][D]

Part Five   Short Answer Questions

81. According to Para. 1, memory plays an important role in _____.

82. We can obviously notice that over a period of no practice what has been learned tends to be forgotten from _____.

83. It seems that the author disagree to explain _____.

84. If memories failed to fade, _____.

85. According to the assumption given in the last para., we don't exactly know _____.

Part Six   Translation

86. _____
87. _____
88. _____
89. _____
90. _____

Model Test 8

Part One Writing

Directions: *For this part, you are allowed thirty minutes to write a composition on the topic* **Lost and Found**. *You should write at least 100 words, and base your composition on the outline (given in Chinese) below:*

1. 假设你是张力,你拾到一个 MP3,想把它归还失主;
2. 拾到 MP3 的时间和地点;
3. MP3 的特征;
4. 你的联系方式。

Part Two Listening Comprehension

Section A

Directions: *In this section you will hear 10 short conversations. At the end of each conversation, a question will be asked about what was said, both the conversation and the question will be spoken only once. After each question there will be a pause. During the pause, you must read the four choices marked A, B, C and D, and decide which is the best answer. Then mark the corresponding letter on the Answer Sheet with a single line through the center.*

1. A. The woman likes the professor's history class very much.

   B. The woman doesn't have any history class.

   C. The woman can hardly understand what the professor says in class.

   D. The woman thinks her history class is interesting.

2. A. She had to go to hospital to see John.

   B. She was hurt in an accident and taken to the hospital.

   C. She went to visit some movie stars instead.

D. She did not like the new movie.

3. A. Some foreign language.

   B. Only English.

   C. Mostly the students' language.

   D. Each language about half the time.

4. A. Because she has an appointment in KFC.

   B. Because she has to go to the English club.

   C. Because she has to work.

   D. Because she does not want to go.

5. A. She is pleased to have some ice-cream.

   B. She does not like ice-cream.

   C. She's had enough already.

   D. She can't have ice-cream because she is trying to lose weight.

6. A. At the railway station.

   B. At the airport.

   C. At the bus terminal.

   D. On the campus.

7. A. He is sure he can pass it.

   B. He will not pass it.

   C. He is worried about it.

   D. He has no idea about it.

8. A. The manager and the secretary.

   B. The teacher and the student.

   C. The salesman and the customer.

   D. The waiter and the customer.

9. A. That he shut the window tightly.

   B. That he put some screws in the wood.

   C. That he stick to his work.

   D. That he use a tool to open the window.

10. A. Call his mother himself.

    B. Find the maid before they leave.

    C. Ask the maid to phone his mother.

    D. Leave for the airport at once.

112

Section B

Directions: *In this section, you will hear three short passages. At the end of each passage, you will hear some questions. Both the passage and the questions will be spoken only once. After you hear a question, you must choose the best answer from the four choices marked A, B, C and D, and decide which is the best answer. Then mark the corresponding letter on the Answer Sheet with a single line through the center.*

Passage 1

Questions 11 to 13 are based on the passage you have just heard.

11. What is one important form of soil conservation?

 A. Farming.

 B. The forces of nature.

 C. The use windbreaks.

 D. Fields.

12. Which is not the function of the windbreaks?

 A. Windbreaks can provide farmers with more food.

 B. Windbreaks stop the wind from blowing soil away.

 C. Windbreaks keep the wind from destroying or damaging crops.

 D. Windbreaks are very important for growing grains, such as wheat.

13. When do windbreaks seem to work best?

 A. When the wall of trees and plants blocks the wind completely.

 B. When they are built around the fields.

 C. When the plants grow well.

 D. When they allow a little wind to pass through.

Passage 2

Questions 14 to 16 are based on the passage you have just heard.

14. A. Because the subjects are too difficult to learn.

 B. Because the subjects are hot.

 C. Because they want to study in "hot" majors.

 D. Because they don't like the subject.

15. A. Foreign languages.

   B. Biology.

   C. Law.

   D. International business.

16. A. Choosing a hot major.

   B. Choosing a scientific major.

   C. Choosing English as a major.

   D. Choosing your major according to your own interests.

Passage 3

Questions 17 to 20 are based on the passage you have just heard.

17. A. 450 billion.

   B. 4050 billion.

   C. 450 million.

   D. 4050 million.

18. A. the United Kingdom.

   B. Canada.

   C. India.

   D. the U.S.

19. A. Old age.

   B. Accidents.

   C. Mental illness.

   D. Attitude.

20. A. They could not get up steps, or on to buses and trains.

   B. They ould not see where you were going or could not hear the traffic.

   C. Ignorance.

   D. Prejudice.

Section C

Directions: *In this section, you will hear a passage of about 100 words three times. The passage is printed on your Answer Sheet with about 10 words missing. First you will hear the whole passage from the beginning to the end just to get a general idea of it. Then, in the second reading, you will hear a signal* *indicating the beginning of a pause after each sentence, sometimes two sentences or just part of a sentence. During the pause, you must write down the missing words you have just heard in the corresponding space on the Answer Sheet. There is also a different signal indicating the end of the pause. When you hear this signal, you must get ready for what comes next from the recording. You can check what you have written when the passage is read to you once again without the pauses.*

A passage with 10 missing words

The keys to a successful homestay __(21)__ are understanding and flexibility. While you or your parents may have decided that a homestay is the best __(22)__ , a homestay is really __(23)__ just a place to stay during your English studies. A homestay __(24)__ that you share living space, the telephone, and __(25)__ with other persons; __(26)__ , you will have to respect __(27)__ of others as well. There will also be __(28)__ that you will have to obey. If you require considerable __(29)__ , a homestay may not be __(30)__ living in an apartment or other kinds of housing.

Part Three Reading Comprehension

Section A

Directions: *In this section, there is a passage with 10 blanks. You are required to select one word for each blank from a list of choices given in a word bank following the passage. Read the passage through carefully before making your choices. Each choice in the bank is identified by a letter. Please mark the corresponding letter for each item on Answer Sheet with a single line through the center.* **You may not use any of words in the bank more than once.**

A passage with 10 blanks

Do you like wearing clothes? If so, you might someday be able to power your gear, like an MP3 player or a cell phone, __(31)__ to electricity created by nothing more than the fibers in your shirt rubbing against each other.

The __(32)__ is embedding tiny wires into fabric, which then use the piezoelectric (压电的)effect to __(33)__ electricity. The piezoelectric effect is one of the oldest electrical technologies __(34)__ to man. It works when pressure is applied to certain materials (in this case gold and zinc oxide rubbing together), causing an electric charge to be generated. The gold captures the charge and can then __(35)__ it into a circuit for use.

Since the amount of __(36)__ required to generate a charge is tiny, the shirt does its work just from being worn __(37)__. Small movements, even a gentle breeze, are plenty to generate a charge. Just put enough nano wires in the shirt, and you've got enough juice to __(38)__ an MP3 player: One square meter of nanowire-laden fabric can potentially produce about 80 milli-watts of __(39)__.

The one drawback is that Zinc oxide(氧化锌)isn't waterproof, so washing is out of the __(40)__, as is getting caught in the rain, lest your power-generating capabilities simply wash away.

A. owe	E. knowing	I. Generate	M. regularly
B. pressure	F. transmit	J. transport	N. known
C. rarely	G. electricity	K. thanks	O. trick
D. question	H. offer	L. recharge	

Section B

Directions: *There are 2 passages in this section. Each passage is followed by some questions or unfinished statements. For each of them there are four choices marked A, B, C and D. You should decide on the best choice and mark the corresponding letter on Answer Sheet with a single line through the center.*

Passage 1

Questions 41 to 45 are based on the following passage.

Reality television is a genre of television programming which, it is claimed, presents unscripted dramatic or humorous situations, documents actual events, and features ordinary people rather than professional actors. It could be described as a form of artificial or "heightened" documentary. Although the genre has existed in some form or another since the early years of television, the current explosion of popularity dates from around 2000.

Critics say that the term "reality television" is somewhat of a misnomer(用词不当) and that such shows frequently portray a modified and highly influenced form of reality, with participants put in exotic(奇异的) locations or abnormal situations, sometimes coached to act in certain ways by off-screen handlers, and with events on screen manipulated(操作) through editing and other post-production techniques.

116

Part of reality television's appeal is due to its ability to place ordinary people in extraordinary situations. For example, on the ABC show, The Bachelor, an eligible male dates a dozen women simultaneously, traveling on extraordinary dates to scenic locations. Reality television also has the potential to turn its participants into national celebrities(名人), outwardly in talent and performance programs such as Pop Idol, though frequently Survivor and Big Brother participants also reach some degree of celebrity.

Some commentators have said that the name "reality television" is an inaccurate description for several styles of program included in the genre(类型). In competition-based programs such as Big Brother and Survivor, and other special-living-environment shows like The Real World, the producers design the format of the show and control the day-to-day activities and the environment, creating a completely fabricated(虚构的) world in which the competition plays out. Producers specifically select the participants, and use carefully designed scenarios(游戏的关), challenges, events, and settings to encourage particular behaviors and conflicts. Mark Burnett, creator of Survivor and other reality shows, has agreed with this assessment, and avoids the word "reality" to describe his shows; he has said, "I tell good stories. It really is not reality TV. It really is unscripted drama."

41. Reality television _____.

    A. has always been this popular

    B. has been popular since well before 2000

    C. has only been popular since 2000

    D. has been popular since approximately 2000

42. Reality TV appeals to some because _____.

    A. it shows eligible males dating women

    B. it uses exotic locations

    C. it shows average people in exceptional circumstances

    D. it can turn ordinary people into celebrities

43. Pop Idol _____.

    A. turns all its participants into celebrities

    B. is more likely to turn its participants into celebrities than Big Brother

    C. is less likely to turn its participants into celebrities than Big Brother

    D. is a dating show

44. Producers choose the participants _____.

    A. on the ground of talent

    B. only for special-living-environment shows

    C. to create conflict among other things

    D. to make a fabricated world

45. Paul Burnett _____.

    A. was a participant on Survivor

    B. is a critic of reality TV

    C. thinks the term "reality television" is inaccurate

    D. writes the script for Survivor

Passage 2

Questions 46 to 50 are based on the following passage.

There's a professor at the University of Toronto in Canada who has come up with a term to describe the way a lot of us North Americans interact these days. And now a big research study confirms it.

Barry Wellman's term is "networked individualism." It's not the easiest concept to grasp. In fact, the words seem to contradict each other. How can we be individualistic and networked at the same time? You need other people for networks.

Here's what he means. Until the Internet and e-mail came along, our social networks involved flesh-and-blood relatives, friends, neighbors, and colleagues at work. Some of the interaction was by phone, but it was still voice to voice, person to person, in real time.

But the latest study by the Pew Internet and American Life Project confirms that for a lot of people, electronic interaction through the computer has replaced a great deal of social interchange. A lot of folks Pew talked with say that's a good thing, because of concerns that the Internet was turning us into hermits who shut out other people in favor of a make-believe world on flickering computer screens.

To the contrary, the Pew study discovered. The Internet has put us in touch with many MORE real people than we'd have ever imagined. Helpful people, too. We're turning to an ever-growing list of cyber friends for advice on careers, medical crises, child-rearing, and choosing a school or college. About 60 million Americans told Pew that the Internet plays an important or crucial role in helping them deal with major life decisions.

118

So we networked individuals are pretty tricky: We're keeping more to ourselves, while at the same time reaching out to more people, all with just the click of a computer mouse!

46. The Pew study was conducted in _____ .

   A. The United States

   B. Canada

   C. The U.S. and Canada

   D. Europe

47. In this article, a network is a group of connected _____ .

   A. radio or TV stations

   B. people

   C. computers

   D. roads

48. Before the invention of the Internet, our connections with people took place mainly

   _____ .

   A. in person

   B. by phone

   C. by letter

   D. by email

49. Which of the following has happened since the invention of the Internet and email?

   A. People are talking on the phone more than ever.

   B. Interaction through the computer has replaced a lot of person to person interaction.

   C. Americans are turning into hermits.

   D. Sixty million Americans have bought computers.

50. Which of the following was NOT one of the discoveries of the Pew study?

   A. The Internet has put us in touch with more people than expected.

   B. People use the Internet to get advice on careers, medical problems, and other questions.

   C. For many Americans, the Internet plays an important role in helping them make important decisions.

   D. "nternet addiction" is a growing problem among people who use computers.

Part Four Vocabulary

Reading involves looking at graphic symbols and formulating mentally the sounds and ideas they represent. Concepts of reading have changed __51__ over the centuries. During the 1950's and 1960's especially, increased attention has been devoted to __52__ the reading process. __53__ specialists agree that reading __54__ a complex organization of higher mental __55__ , they disagree __56__ the exact nature of the process. Some experts, who regard language primarily as a code using symbols to represent sounds, __57__ reading as simply the decoding of symbols into the sounds they stand __58__ .

These authorities __59__ that meaning, being concerned with thinking, must be taught independently of the decoding process. Others maintain that reading is __60__ related to thinking, and that a child who pronounces sounds without __61__ their meaning is not truly reading. The reader, __62__ some, is not just a person with a theoretical ability to read but one who __63__ reads.

Many adults, although they have the ability to read, have never read a book in its __64__ . By some expert they would not be __65__ as readers. Clearly, the philosophy, objectives, methods and materials of reading will depend on the definition one use. By the most __66__ and satisfactory definition, reading is the ability to __67__ the sound-symbols code of the language, to interpret meaning for various __68__ , at various rates, and at various levels of difficulty, and to do __69__ widely and enthusiastically. __70__ reading is the interpretation of ideas through the use of symbols representing sounds and ideas.

51. A. substantively   B. substantially   C. substitutely   D. subjectively

52. A. define and describe   B. definition and description
    C. defining and describing   D. have defined and described

53. A. Although.   B. If   C. Unless   D. Until

54. A. involves   B. involves to   C. is involved   D. involves of

55. A. opinions   B. effects   C. manners   D. functions

56. A. of   B. about   C. for   D. into

57. A. view   B. look   C. reassure   D. agree

58. A. by   B . to   C. off   D. for

59. A. content   B. contend   C. contempt   D. contact

120

60. A. inexplicably   B. inexpressible
    C. inextricably   D. inexpediently
61. A. interpreting   B. saying   C. explaining   D. reading
62. A. like   B. for example   C. according to   D. as
63. A. sometimes   B. might   C. practical   D. actually
64. A. entire   B. entirety   C. entirely   D. entity
65. A. classed   B. granted   C. classified   D. graded
66. A. inclusive   B. inclinable   C. conclusive   D. complicated
67. A. break up   B. elaborate   C. define   D. unlock
68. A. purposes   B. degrees   C. stages   D. steps
69. A. such   B. so as   C. so   D. such as
70. A. By the way   B. In short
    C. So far   D. On the other hand

Part Five   Short Answer Questions

Directions: *In this part there is a short passage with five questions or incomplete state-*
        ments. Read the passage carefully. Then answer the questions or complete
        the statement in the fewest possible words.

Questions 71 to 75 are based on the following passage.

There are two factors which determine an individual's intelligence. The first is the sort of brain he is born with. Human brains differ considerably, some being more capable than others. But no matter how good a brain he has to begin with, an individual will have a low order of intelligence unless he has opportunities to learn. So the second factor is what happens to the individual—the sort of environment in which he is reared. If an individual is handicapped environmentally, it is likely that his brain will fail to develop and he will never attain the level of intelligence of which he is capable.

The importance of environment in determining an individual's intelligence can be demonstrated by the case history of the identical twins, Peter and Mark X. Being identical, the twins had identical brains at birth, and their growth processes were the same. When the twins were three months old, their parents died, and they were placed in separate foster homes. Peter was related by parents of low intelligence in an isolated community with poor educational opportunities. Mark was reared in the home of well-to-do parents who had been to college. He was read to as a child, sent to good schools, and given every opportunity to be stimulated intellectually. This environmental difference continued until the twins were in their late teens, when they were given tests to measure their intelligence. Mark's I. Q. was 125, twenty-five points higher than the average and fully forty points higher than his identical brother. Given equal opportunities, the twins, having identical brains, would have tested at roughly the same level.

71. What are the two factors which determine an individual's intelligence?

72. What is crucial in determining a person's intelligence?

73. According to the passage, what is the average I. Q. ?

74. What is the conclusion drawn from the case history of the twins appears?

75. What's the best title for this passage?

Part Six   Translation

Directions: *Finish the sentences on Answer Sheet by translating into English* .

76. We were told _____(匹萨 20 分钟后送来).

77. Theory is based on practice and _____(反过来为实践服务).

78. The magistrate dismissed the case _____ (由于缺乏证据).

79. It is essential that he _____ (明天让人把洗衣机修好).

80. According to the schedule, the train to Shen Zhen _____(定于上午 10 点钟发车).

81. The company was in great difficulty at the end of last year, _____ (但银行的一大笔贷款使它渡过了难关).

82. We'll have our soccer game _____(除非天气下雨).

83. _____ (桥上的交通阻塞了几个小时) because of the accident.

84. The doctors decided _____ (尽可能快地给他动手术).

85. _____ (他从事教书) at 22 and became quite experienced later.

Answer Sheet

Part One   Writing

Lost and Found

_____

_____

_____

_____

_____

_____

_____

_____

_____

_____

_____

_____

_____

_____

_____

_____

_____

_____

_____

_____

_____

_____

Part Two　Listening Comprehension

Section A

1. [A][B][C][D]　2. [A][B][C][D]　3. [A][B][C][D]　4. [A][B][C][D]
5. [A][B][C][D]　6. [A][B][C][D]　7. [A][B][C][D]　8. [A][B][C][D]
9. [A][B][C][D]　10. [A][B][C][D]

Section B

11. [A][B][C][D] 12. [A][B][C][D]　13. [A][B][C][D]　14. [A][B][C][D]
15. [A][B][C][D] 16. [A][B][C][D]　17. [A][B][C][D]　18. [A][B][C][D]
19. [A][B][C][D] 20. [A][B][C][D]

Section C

21. _____　22. _____　23. _____　24. _____
25. _____　26. _____　27. _____　28. _____
29. _____　　30. _____

Part Three　Reading Comprehension

Section A　　　　　　　　　　　　　　　　　　　　Section B

31. [A][B][C][D][E][F][G][H][I][J][K][L][M][N][O]　41. [A][B][C][D]
32. [A][B][C][D][E][F][G][H][I][J][K][L][M][N][O]　42. [A][B][C][D]
33. [A][B][C][D][E][F][G][H][I][J][K][L][M][N][O]　43. [A][B][C][D]
34. [A][B][C][D][E][F][G][H][I][J][K][L][M][N][O]　44. [A][B][C][D]
35. [A][B][C][D][E][F][G][H][I][J][K][L][M][N][O]　45. [A][B][C][D]
36. [A][B][C][D][E][F][G][H][I][J][K][L][M][N][O]　46. [A][B][C][D]
37. [A][B][C][D][E][F][G][H][I][J][K][L][M][N][O]　47. [A][B][C][D]
38. [A][B][C][D][E][F][G][H][I][J][K][L][M][N][O]　48. [A][B][C][D]
39. [A][B][C][D][E][F][G][H][I][J][K][L][M][N][O]　49. [A][B][C][D]
40. [A][B][C][D][E][F][G][H][I][J][K][L][M][N][O]　50. [A][B][C][D]

Part Four　Vocabulary

51. [A][B][C][D] 52. [A][B][C][D]　53. [A][B][C][D]　54. [A][B][C][D]

55. [A][B][C][D] 56. [A][B][C][D] 57. [A][B][C][D] 58. [A][B][C][D]
59. [A][B][C][D] 60. [A][B][C][D] 61. [A][B][C][D] 62. [A][B][C][D]
63. [A][B][C][D] 64. [A][B][C][D] 65. [A][B][C][D] 66. [A][B][C][D]
67. [A][B][C][D] 68. [A][B][C][D] 69. [A][B][C][D] 70. [A][B][C][D]

Part Five   Short Answer Questions

71. What are the two factors which determine an individual's intelligence?

_____

72. What is crucial in determining a person's intelligence?

_____

73. According to the passage, what is the average I. Q. ?

_____

74. What is the conclusion drawn from the case history of the twins appears?

_____

_____

75. What's the best title for this passage?

_____

Part Six   Translation

76. _____
77. _____
78. _____
79. _____
80. _____
81. _____
82. _____
83. _____
84. _____
85. _____

Model Test 9

Part One   Writing

Directions: *For this part, you are allowed thirty minutes to write a composition on the topic* **On Campus Lectures**. *You should write at least 100 words, and base your composition on the outline (given in Chinese) below:*

1. 大学校园里经常开设各类讲座；
2. 听讲座的益处；
3. 你的看法。

Part Two   Listening Comprehension

Section A

Directions: *In this section you will hear 10 short conversations. At the end of each conversation, a question will be asked about what was said, both the conversation and the question will be spoken only once. After each question there will be a pause. During the pause, you must read the four choices marked A, B, C and D, and decide which is the best answer. Then mark the corresponding letter on the Answer Sheet with a single line through the center.*

1. A. Play football with her.
   B. Watch a football game on TV with her.
   C. Take her to a football game.
   D. Pick her up for a movie.

2. A. The woman wants to eat out with the man.
   B. The woman doesn't like to eat out with the man.
   C. The woman likes to stay at home for dinner.
   D. The woman has had her dinner.

3. A. His proposal was accepted last week.

   B. He was not sure whether his proposal was accepted or not.

   C. He lost his proposal last week.

   D. His proposal was refused last week.

4. A. In an office.   B. In a hotel.

   C. In a restaurant.   D. In a cinema.

5. A. The manager and the secretary.

   B. The teacher and the student.

   C. The salesman and the customer.

   D. The waiter and the customer.

6. A. The woman should buy some clothes.

   B. The woman should buy some clothes of a larger size.

   C. The woman should eat less.

   D. The woman should do more exercises.

7. A. He's willing to lend his laptop.

   B. He doesn't have a laptop.

   C. He refuses to lend the woman his laptop.

   D. He lent his laptop to someone else.

8. A. The man is not sure if John has rung him.

   B. The man knows John, but not very well.

   C. The name sounds familiar to the man.

   D. The man doesn't know John at all.

9. A. The man is reviewing Japanese.

   B. The man is speaking Japanese.

   C. The man is working for his doctor degree.

   D. The man is staying in Japan.

10. A. 6:30.   B. 6:25.   C. 5:50.   D. 5:55.

Section B

Directions: *In this section, you will hear three short passages. At the end of each passage, you will hear some questions. Both the passage and the questions will be spoken only once. After you hear a question, you must choose the best answer from the four choices marked A, B, C and D, and decide which is the* *best answer. Then mark the corresponding letter on the Answer Sheet with a single line through the center.*

Passage 1

Questions 11 to 13 are based on the passage you have just heard.

11. A. 70% of the UK households.　　B. 44% of the UK households.
　　C. 50% of the UK households.　　D. 11.2% of the UK households.
12. A. Because of the cost.　　　　　B. Because of the internet speeds.
　　C. Because of lack of computers.　D. Because of lack of skills.
13. A. It is going down.　　　　　　 B. It is increasing.
　　C. It isn't changing.　　　　　　 D. It is very cheap.

Passage 2

Questions 14 to 16 are based on the passage you have just heard.

14. A. Cats and dogs.　　　　　　　 B. Dogs and fish.
　　C. Cats and monkeys.　　　　　　D. Birds and fish.
15. A. Because they love pets very much.
　　B. Because they take pets as part of their families.
　　C. Because they believe pets have rights to be treated kindly.
　　D. Because they think pets are precious property to them.
16. A. Because it prepares them for shouldering responsibility.
　　B. Because it facilitates them to improve their relationship.
　　C. Because it is easier for them to communicate with their neighbors.
　　D. Because it makes their family life more interesting.

Passage 3

Questions 17 to 20 are based on the passage you have just heard.

17. A. Seeds and Insects.　　　　　　B. Grains.
　　C. High-fat junk food.　　　　　 D. Low-fat food.
18. A. The city council.　　　　　　　B. Everyone who feeds the pigeons.
　　C. The tourists.　　　　　　　　　D. The pigeon keepers.
19. A. Visitors have been warned not to go there.
　　B. Big birds have been brought there.

128

C. Tourists have been asked to make noises.

D. Robotic birds have been brought into the city centre.

20. A. Liverpool.   B. London.   C. Edinburgh.   D. Manchester.

Section C

Directions: *In this section, you will hear a passage of about 100 words three times. The passage is printed on your Answer Sheet with about 10 words missing. First you will hear the whole passage from the beginning to the end just to get a general idea of it. Then, in the second reading, you will hear a signal indicating the beginning of a pause after each sentence, sometimes two sentences or just part of a sentence. During the pause, you must write down the missing words you have just heard in the corresponding space on the Answer Sheet. There is also a different signal indicating the end of the pause. When you hear this signal, you must get ready for what comes next from the recording. You can check what you have written when the passage is read to you once again without the pauses.*

A passage with 10 missing words

The   (21)   of Japan's prized sport, sumo wrestling, is in   (22)   after three sumo wrestlers and a stable   (23)   were arrested in February, 2008, following an alleged hazing   (24) . A 17-year old wrestler died the summer before, after collapsing in his sumo stable. Policemen later   (25)   that the boy died of   (26)   after being badly beaten during   (27) . Stable master, Junichi Yamamoto and three sumo wrestlers are facing   (28) . Police believe Yamamoto   (29)   and ordered the beating after he   (30) .

Part Three   Reading Comprehension

Section A

Directions: *In this section, there is a passage with 10 blanks. You are required to select one word for each blank from a list of choices given in a word bank following the passage. Read the passage through carefully before making your choices. Each choice in the bank is identified by a letter. Please mark the*

A passage with 10 blanks

Albert Einstein once __(31)__ the creativity of a famous scientist to the __(32)__ that he "never went to school, and therefore preserved the rare __(33)__ of thinking freely." There is undoubtedly truth in Einstein's observation; many artists and geniuses seem to view their __(34)__ as a disadvantage. But such a truth is not a __(35)__ of schools. It is the function of schools to civilize, not to train explorers. The __(36)__ is always a lonely individual whether his or her pioneering be in art, music, science, or technology. The creative explorer of unmapped lands __(37)__ with the genius what William James described as the "faculty of perceiving in an unhabitual way." Insofar as schools teach perceptual patterns they tend to __(38)__ creativity and genius. But if schools could somehow exist solely to cultivate genius, then society would break down. For the social order __(39)__ unity and widespread agreement, both traits are destructive to creativity. There will always be __(40)__ between the demands of society and the impulses of creativity and genius.

Word Bank

A. demands	E. criticism	I. conflict	M. schooling
B. contributed	F. science	J. that	N. critical
C. shares	G. gift	K. destroy	O. fact
D. school	H. attributed	L. explorer	

Section B

Directions: *There are 2 passages in this section. Each passage is followed by some questions or unfinished statements. For each of them there are four choices marked A, B, C and D. You should decide on the best choice and mark the corresponding letter on Answer Sheet with a single line through the center.*

Passage 1

Questions 41 to 45 are based on the following passage.

Pictures from outer space now show us how much land has changed on earth. These images are taken by Landsat 7, a government satellite. The satellites have been used for

27 years. They reveal the clear-cutting of forests in the northwestern part of the United States. Pictures show the loss of rain forests in South America.

NASA's Darrel Williams speaks about the Landsat 7 Project. He said that an eruption caused trees to burn up in a large forest. Fifteen years later, pinkish images from space show that the trees and plant life are growing again. Williams says that clear-cut areas easily show up in the pictures. He wants Americans to look at how much land is being cleared of forests in our country.

Satellites have provided other information about changes on earth. In the past ten years, more than four miles have shrunk from glaciers in Alaska. Landsat 7 received these computer images of Glacier Bay in Alaska.

Hurricanes Floyd and Irene have damaged the coastline in North Carolina. Runoff from farms and silt have gone into the ocean according to satellite images. Loss of trees and forests have caused hotter summers in southern cities such as Atlanta, Georgia.

The Landsat 7 images are like pictures in a photo album. Instead of pictures of the family, the album shows changes around the globe in the past 25 years.

A new satellite, Terra, is going to be launched by NASA soon. It will be more advanced that Landsat 7 and will take important global pictures. Ocean temperatures and energy loss will be provided by Terra daily.

41. Landsat 7 shows how changes have occurred on land by sending back _____.
    A. images taken with a Polaroid camera
    B. the latest images taken by a government satellite
    C. a television camera
    D. astronauts

42. NASA can tell that vegetation is growing back because of _____.
    A. a bright, white light that is reflected
    B. little tiny trees that are growing
    C. vegetable gardens that are planted
    D. a light, pinkish view from space

43. Landsat 7 knows that Alaskan glaciers have shrunk because _____.
    A. sightseers have noted the changes
    B. computer-animated views have shown the shrinkage
    C. one of the glaciers was hit by a ship

D. the temperatures are much colder

44. Silt and heavy run-off from farms in North Carolina were caused by _____.

   A. hurricanes Irene and Floyd

   B. hurricanes Floyd and Carla

   C. an eruption from a volcano

   D. deforestation of trees

45. Terra will be a better satellite because _____.

   A. no other country can make one like it

   B. it is much cheaper to operate

   C. it is more sophisticated than Landsat 7

   D. Terra will show energy gains

Passage 2

Questions 46 to 50 are based on the following passage.

College graduation brings both the satisfaction of academic achievement and the expectation of a well-paying job.

But for 6000 graduates at San Jose State this year, there's uncertainty as they enter one of the worst job markets in decades. Ryan Stewart has a freshly minted degree in religious studies, but no job prospects.

"You look at everybody's parents and neighbors, and they're getting laid off and don't have jobs," said Stewart. "Then you look at the young people just coming into the workforce. . . it's just scary. "

When the class of 2003 entered college the future never looked brighter. But in the four years they've been here, the world outside has changed dramatically.

"Those were the exciting times, lots of dot-com opportunities, exploding offers, students getting top dollar with lots of benefits," said Cheryl Allmen-Vinnidge, of the San Jose State Career Center. "Times have changed. It's a new market. "

Cheryl Allmen-Vinnidge ought to know. She runs the San Jose State Career Center (it is) sort of a crossroads between college and the real world. Allmen-Vinnidge says students who do find jobs after college have done their homework.

"The typical graduate who does have a job offer started working on it two years ago. They've postured themselves well during the summer. They've had several internships," she said.

132

And they've majored in one of the few fields that are still hot—like chemical engineering, accounting, or nursing—where average starting salaries have actually increased over last year. Other popular fields (like information systems management, computer science, and political science) have seen big declines in starting salaries.

Ryan Stewart (he had hoped to become a teacher) may just end up going back to school.

"I'd like to teach college some day and that requires more schooling, which would be great in a bad economy," he said.

To some students a degree may not be ticket to instant wealth. For now, they can only hope its value will, increase over time.

46. This story mentions college graduates at _____.

A. San Jose State Career Center

B. San Jose Community College

C. San Jose State University

D. San Jose Polytechnic High School

47. The main idea of this story is that _____.

A. Ryan Stewart has not been able to find a job

B. a college career center is a crossroads between college and the real world

C. in some fields, salaries have increased in the past year

D. between 1999 and 2003, the job market changed dramatically

48. Ryan Stewart _____.

A. is a teacher

B. found a job as soon as he graduated

C. majored in religious studies

D. is going back to school

49. Which of the following things did not happen in the four years that the class of 2003 was in college?

A. Dot-Com opportunities decreased.

B. The number of teaching jobs increased.

C. Salaries in chemical engineering increased.

D. The number of jobs with benefits decreased.

50. Which of the following majors has the best job prospects, according to the story?

A. Information systems management.   B. Accounting.

C. Computer science.   D. Teaching.

Part Four   Vocabulary

    (51)   Between men and women results in poorer health for children and greater   (52)   for the family,   (53)   to a new study. The UN agency UNICEF found that in places where women are   (54)   from family decisions, children are more likely to suffer from   (55)   . There would be 13 million   (56)   malnourished children in South Asia if women had an equal say in the family, UNICEF said.

    UNICEF   (57)   family decision-making in 30 countries   (58)   the world. Their chief finding is that equality between men and women is vital to   (59)   poverty and improving health, especially that of children, in developing   (60)   . The conclusions are contained in the agency's latest report. This report   (61)   to a greater   (62)   of opportunities for girls and women in education and work which contributes to disempowerment and poverty. Where men control the household, less money   (63)   health care and food for the family, which   (64)   in poorer health for the children.

    An increase in   (65)   and income-earning opportunities for women would increase their   (66)   power, the report   (67)   . For example, the   (68)   found that   (69)   has the greater share of household income and assets decides whether those   (70)   will be used for family needs.

51. A. Unequal   B. Inequal   C. Unequality   D. Inequality
52. A. poor   B. poorness   C. poverty   D. impoverished
53. A. resulting   B. according   C. regarding   D. with regard
54. A. excluded   B. exclude   C. exclusion   D. excludes
55. A. ill-nourished   B. malnourish   C. malnutrition   D. ill-nutrition
56. A. more   B. few   C. fewer   D. least
57. A. survey   B. surveying   C. surveys   D. surveyed
58. A. in   B. around   C. over   D. among
59. A. increase   B. reduce   C. increasing   D. reducing
60. A. countries   B. powers   C. nations   D. states
61. A. indicates   B. points   C. shows   D. suggests

134

62. A. lack   B. lacking   C. lacks   D. lacky
63. A. is spending on   B. is spent on   C. spends on   D. spent
64. A. leads   B. result   C. lead   D. results
65. A. employ   B. employment   C. employee   D. employed
66. A. house   B. householder   C. household   D. home
67. A. said   B. saying   C. speaks   D. put
68. A. agent   B. agenda   C. agents   D. agency
69. A. whatever   B. whoever   C. whichever   D. however
70. A. resolutions   B. sources   C. resources   D. sauces

Part Five   Short Answer Questions

Directions: *In this part there is a short passage with five questions or incomplete state-ments. Read the passage carefully. Then answer the questions or complete the statement in the fewest possible words.*

Questions 71 to 75 are based on the following passage.

The United States is on the verge of losing its leading place in the world's technology. So says more than one study in recent years. One of the reasons for this decline is the parallel decline in the number of U. S. scientists and engineers.

Since 1976, employment of scientists and engineers is up 85 percent. This trend is expected to continue. However, the trend shows that the number of 22-year-olds—the near term source of future PH.D. s—is declining. Further adding to the problem is the increased competition for these candidates from other fields-law, medicine, business, etc. While the number of U. S. PH. D. s in science and engineering declines, the award of PH. D. s to foreign nationals is increasing rapidly.

Our inability to motivate students to pursue science and engineering careers at the graduate level is compounded because of the intense demand industry has for bright Bachelor's and Master's degree holders. Too often, promising PH. D. candidates, con-fronting the cost and financial sacrifice of pursuing their education, find the attraction of industry irresistible.

71. Why will the U. S. come to lose its leading place in technology?

72. The field of science and engineering is facing a competition from _____.

73. What do Large-scale enterprises now need?

74. Why do many promising postgraduates are unwilling to pursue a PH. D. degree?

75. PH. D. candidates "find the attraction of industry irresistible" means that _____ .

Part Six   Translation

Directions: *Finish the sentences on Answer Sheet by translating into English.*

76. His mother is constantly _____ (挑他的毛病).

77. _____(结清所有的账目之后), he found that he has got more than 2000 yuan left.

78. It is evident that the local government will _____(干预这件事情) and solve the problem properly.

79. The delegation is _____ (由商人和公务员组成).

80. Not until he graduated from the college _____ (那个年轻人才独立).

81. _____(即使你不喜欢英语), you have to work hard at it in order to pass the exam.

82. If I had a lot of money, _____ (我就买了那辆汽车) last year.

83. The girl _____(很敏感) what people say about her appearance.

84. The more you explain, _____ (我愈糊涂).

85. _____ (众所周知), water is composed of hydrogen and oxygen.

Answer Sheet

Part One   Writing

On Campus Lectures

_____

_____

_____

_____

_____

_____

_____

_____

_____

_____

_____

_____

_____

_____

_____

_____

_____

_____

_____

_____

_____

_____

Part Two Listening Comprehension

Section A

1. [A][B][C][D]   2. [A][B][C][D]   3. [A][B][C][D]   4. [A][B][C][D]
5. [A][B][C][D]   6. [A][B][C][D]   7. [A][B][C][D]   8. [A][B][C][D]
9. [A][B][C][D]   10. [A][B][C][D]

Section B

11. [A][B][C][D]   12. [A][B][C][D]   13. [A][B][C][D]   14. [A][B][C][D]
15. [A][B][C][D]   16. [A][B][C][D]   17. [A][B][C][D]   18. [A][B][C][D]
19. [A][B][C][D]   20. [A][B][C][D]

Section C

21. _____   22. _____   23. _____   24. _____

25. _____   26. _____   27. _____

28. _____   29. _____

30. _____

Part Three Reading Comprehension

Section A   Section B

31. [A][B][C][D][E][F][G][H][I][J][K][L][M][N][O]   41. [A][B][C][D]
32. [A][B][C][D][E][F][G][H][I][J][K][L][M][N][O]   42. [A][B][C][D]
33. [A][B][C][D][E][F][G][H][I][J][K][L][M][N][O]   43. [A][B][C][D]
34. [A][B][C][D][E][F][G][H][I][J][K][L][M][N][O]   44. [A][B][C][D]
35. [A][B][C][D][E][F][G][H][I][J][K][L][M][N][O]   45. [A][B][C][D]
36. [A][B][C][D][E][F][G][H][I][J][K][L][M][N][O]   46. [A][B][C][D]
37. [A][B][C][D][E][F][G][H][I][J][K][L][M][N][O]   47. [A][B][C][D]
38. [A][B][C][D][E][F][G][H][I][J][K][L][M][N][O]   48. [A][B][C][D]
39. [A][B][C][D][E][F][G][H][I][J][K][L][M][N][O]   49. [A][B][C][D]
40. [A][B][C][D][E][F][G][H][I][J][K][L][M][N][O]   50. [A][B][C][D]

Part Four Vocabulary

51. [A][B][C][D]   52. [A][B][C][D]   53. [A][B][C][D]   54. [A][B][C][D]

55. [A][B][C][D] 56. [A][B][C][D] 57. [A][B][C][D] 58. [A][B][C][D]
59. [A][B][C][D] 60. [A][B][C][D] 61. [A][B][C][D] 62. [A][B][C][D]
63. [A][B][C][D] 64. [A][B][C][D] 65. [A][B][C][D] 66. [A][B][C][D]
67. [A][B][C][D] 68. [A][B][C][D] 69. [A][B][C][D] 70. [A][B][C][D]

Part Five   Short Answer Questions

71. Why will the U. S. come to lose its leading place in technology?

_____

72. The field of science and engineering is facing a competition from

_____

73. What do Large-scale enterprises now need?

_____

74. Why do many promising postgraduates are unwilling to pursue a PH. D. degree?

_____

75. PH. D. candidates "find the attraction of industry irresistible" means that

_____

Part Six   Translation

76. _____
77. _____
78. _____
79. _____
80. _____
81. _____
82. _____
83. _____
84. _____
85. _____

Model Test 10

Part One　Writing

Directions: *For this part, you are allowed thirty minutes to write a composition on the topic **Jobs for Graduates**. You should write at least 100 words, and base your composition on the outline (given in Chinese) below:*

1. 大学生难找工作；
2. 原因很多；
3. 解决的办法。

Part Two　Listening Comprehension

Section A

Directions: *In this section you will hear 10 short conversations. At the end of each conversation, a question will be asked about what was said, both the conversation and the question will be spoken only once. After each question there will be a pause. During the pause, you must read the four choices marked A, B, C and D, and decide which is the best answer. Then mark the corresponding letter on the Answer Sheet with a single line through the center.*

1. A. The manager and the secretary.　　B. The teacher and the student.
   C. The salesman and the customer.　　D. The husband and wife.

2. A. At the railway station.　　B. At the airport.
   C. At the bus terminal.　　D. On the campus.

3. A. She's afraid to work at night.
   B. She doesn't want to work tomorrow night.
   C. She wants to get out of KFC.
   D. She's afraid the work there will be tiring.

140

4. A. She hasn't got a partner yet.

    B. She is too busy to work on her Chinese.

    C. She prefers Chinese.

    D. She's too tired of Chinese.

5. A. She didn't go to the interview.

    B. She succeeded in the interview.

    C. She forgot about the interview.

    D. She was too nervous in the interview.

6. A. He feels they have done a wise thing.

    B. He doesn't think they should move.

    C. He thinks it is better to invest later.

    D. He thinks it is unwise to buy stocks.

7. A. It was a long lecture, but easy to understand.

    B. It was not as easy as he had thought.

    C. It was as difficult as he had expected.

    D. It was interesting and easy to follow.

8. A. He got home before 9 o'clock.

    B. He had a bad cold.

    C. He was delayed.

    D. He had a car accident.

9. A. The train is crowded.

    B. The train is late.

    C. The train is empty.

    D. The train is on time.

10. A. James' phone wasn't working.

    B. James wasn't at home when he called.

    C. The man didn't get James' phone number right.

    D. James was too busy to come.

Section B

Directions: *In this section, you will hear three short passages. At the end of each passage, you will hear some questions. Both the passage and the questions will be spoken only once. After you hear a question, you must choose the best an-*

swer from the four choices marked A, B, C and D, and decide which is the best answer. Then mark the corresponding letter on the Answer Sheet with a single line through the center.

Passage 1

Questions 11 to 13 are based on the passage you have just heard.

11. A. To keep fish alive.　　　　　B. To punish criminals.
    C. To preserve dead bodies.　　D. To help heal wounds.

12. A. For stealing salt.　　　　　B. For making salted fish.
    C. For taking salt from the king's table.　D. For selling salt.

13. A. On the king's seat.　　　　　B. In front of the king.
    C. A long way from the important guests.　D. In front of everyone.

Passage 2

Questions 14 to 16 are based on the passage you have just heard.

14. A. To help them to be more healthy.
    B. To improve their intelligence and intellectual performance.
    C. To take the place of coffee or tea.
    D. To be as strong as the athletes.

15. A. To take warming up tests.　　B. To test their intelligence.
    C. To take medical tests.　　　D. To take drugs tests.

16. A. Vitamins.　　B. Drugs.　　C. Pills.　　D. Tablets.

Passage 3

Questions 17 to 20 are based on the passage you have just heard.

17. A. The Fat Duck restaurant.
    B. The Experimental restaurant.
    C. The British Duck restaurant.
    D. The Bacon and Egg restaurant.

18. A. Because you can smoke it.　　B. Because you can eat it.
    C. Because you can chew it.　　D. Because you can smell it.

19. A. Its good food.　　　　　　B. Its cooking.
    C. Its good cuisine.　　　　　D. Its bad food.

20. A. A customer.　　　　　　　　B. A cook.

　　C. A journalist.　　　　　　　D. A restaurant owner.

Section C

Directions: *In this section, you will hear a passage of about 100 words three times. The passage is printed on your Answer Sheet with about 10 words missing. First you will hear the whole passage from the beginning to the end just to get a general idea of it. Then, in the second reading, you will hear a signal indicating the beginning of a pause after each sentence, sometimes two sentences or just part of a sentence. During the pause, you must write down the missing words you have just heard in the corresponding space on the Answer Sheet. There is also a different signal indicating the end of the pause. When you hear this signal, you must get ready for what comes next from the recording. You can check what you have written when the passage is read to you once again without the pauses.*

A passage with 10 missing words

　　When Americans go abroad, one of their biggest ___(21)___ is, "Can you drink the water?" You may find asking yourself the same question, ___(22)___ in a hip, urban setting where you may notice many people, young and old, drinking from large and small ___(23)___ . And these people will tell you, fiercely to put the fear of God in you, that "No! You cannot drink the ___(24)___ in this country anymore!"

　　___(25)___ these people. These are the same kind of people who will also ___(26)___ you that you will drop dead before 40, or worse, become ugly, fat, and stupid if you ___(27)___ where you pay to ___(28)___ . Now simply turn the tap water and drink long and deep ___(29)___ . Do not be surprised the next morning if you still ___(30)___ .

Part Three　Reading Comprehension

Section A

Directions: *In this section, there is a passage with 10 blanks. You are required to select one word for each blank from a list of choices given in a word bank following the passage. Read the passage through carefully before making your choices. Each choice in the bank is identified by a letter. Please mark the* *corresponding letter for each item on Answer Sheet with a single line through the center. **You may not use any of words in the bank more than once.***

A passage with 10 blanks

   (31)   television has both the advantages and disadvantages. In the first place, television is not only a convenient   (32)   of entertainment, but also a comparatively cheap one. With a TV set in the family people don't have to pay for expensive   (33)   at the theatre, the cinema, or the opera. All they have to do is to push a button or turn a knob, and they can see plays, films, operas and   (34)   of every kind. Some people, however, think that this is where the danger lies. The television viewers need to do nothing. He does not even have to use his legs if he has a remote control. He makes no   (35)   and exercises no judgment. He is completely   (36)   and has everything presented to him without any effort on his part.

   Television, it is often said, keeps one   (37)   about current events and the latest developments in science and politics. The most distant countries and the strangest   (38)   are brought right into one's sitting room. It could be argued that the radio performs this service as well; but on television everything is much more living, much more real. Yet here again there is a   (39) . The television screen itself has a terrible, almost physical charm for us. We get so used to looking at the movements on it, so dependent on its pictures,   (40)   it begins to control our lives. People are often heard to say that their television sets have broken down and that they have suddenly found that they have far more time to do things and that they have actually begun to talk to each other again. It makes one think, doesn't it?

   There are many other arguments for and against television. We must realize that television in itself is neither good nor bad. It is the use to which it is put that determines its value to society.

Word Bank

A. as	E. danger	I. Especially	M. shows
B. passive	F. source	J. seats	N. informed
C. display	G. sauce	K. that	O. difficult
D. choice	H. Obviously	L. customs	

Section B

Directions: *There are 2 passages in this section. Each passage is followed by some ques-*

tions or unfinished statements. For each of them there are four choices marked A, B, C and D. You should decide on the best choice and mark the corresponding letter on Answer Sheet with a single line through the center.

Passage 1

Questions 41 to 45 are based on the following passage.

Before the grass has thickened on the roadside verges and leaves have started growing on the trees is a perfect time to look around and see just how dirty Britain has become. The pavements are stained with chewing gum that has been spat out and the gutters are full of discarded fast food cartons. Years ago I remember traveling abroad and being saddened by the plastic bags, discarded bottles and soiled nappies at the edge of every road. Nowadays, Britain seems to look at least as bad. What has gone wrong?

The problem is that the rubbish created by our increasingly mobile lives lasts a lot longer than before. If it is not cleared up and properly thrown away, it stays in the undergrowth for years; a semi-permanent reminder of what a tatty little country we have now.

Firstly, it is estimated that 10 billion plastic bags have been given to shoppers. These will take anything from 100 to 1,000 years to rot. However, it is not as if there is no solution to this. A few years ago, the Irish government introduced a tax on non-recyclable carrier bags and in three months reduced their use by 90%. When he was a minister, Michael Meacher attempted to introduce a similar arrangement in Britain. The plastics industry protested, of course. However, they need not have bothered; the idea was killed before it could draw breath, leaving supermarkets free to give away plastic bags.

What is clearly necessary right now is some sort of combined initiative, both individual and collective, before it is too late. The alternative is to continue sliding downhill until we have a country that looks like a vast municipal rubbish tip. We may well be at the tipping point. Yet we know that people respond to their environment. If things around them are clean and tidy, people behave cleanly and tidily. If they are surrounded by squalor, they behave squalidly. Now, much of Britain looks pretty squalid. What will it look like in five years?

41. The writer says that it is a good time to see Britain before the trees have leaves because _____.

145

A. Britain looks perfect

B. you can see Britain at its dirtiest

C. you can see how dirty Britain is now

D. the grass has thickened on the verges

42. For the writer, the problem is that _____.

A. rubbish is not cleared up

B. rubbish last longer than it used to

C. our society is increasingly mobile

D. Britain is an old country

43. Michael Meacher _____.

A. followed the Irish example with a tax on plastic bags

B. tried to follow the Irish example with a tax on plastic bags

C. made no attempt to follow the Irish example with a tax on plastic bags

D. had problems with the plastics industry who weren't bothered about the tax

44. The writer thinks _____.

A. it is too late to do anything

B. we are at the tipping point

C. there is no alternative

D. we need to work together to solve the problem

45. The writer thinks that _____.

A. people are squalid

B. people behave according to what they see around them

C. people are clean and tidy

D. people are like a vast municipal rubbish tip

Passage 2

Questions 46 to 50 are based on the following passage.

Leading investors have joined the growing chorus of concern about governments and companies rushing into producing bio-fuels as a solution for global warming, saying that many involved in the sector could be jeopardizing future profits if they do not consider the long-term impact of what they are doing carefully.

It is essential to build sustainability criteria into the supply chain of any green fuel project in order to ensure that there is no adverse effect on the surrounding environment

146

and social structures. The report produced by the investors expresses concern that many companies may not be fully aware of the potential pitfalls in the bio-fuel sector.

Production of corn and soy beans has increased dramatically in the last years as an eco-friendly alternative to fossil fuels but environmental and human rights campaigners are worried that this will lead to destruction of rain forests. Food prices could also go up as there is increased competition for crops as both foodstuffs and sources of fuel. Last week, the UN warned that bio-fuels could have dangerous side effects and said that steps need to be taken to make sure that land converted to grow bio-fuels does not damage the environment or cause civil unrest. There is already great concern about palm oil, which is used in many foods in addition to being an important bio-fuel, as rain forests are being cleared in some countries and people driven from their homes to create palm oil plantations.

An analyst and author of the investors' report says that bio-fuels are not a cure for climate change but they can play their part as long as governments and companies manage the social and environmental impacts thoroughly. There should also be greater measure taken to increase efficiency and to reduce demand.

46. _____ are worried about the boom in bio-fuels.

    A. Few people   B. Many people

    C. Only these leading investors   D. A few people

47. Environmentalists believe that increased production of corn and soy _____.

    A. has destroyed rain forests

    B. may lead to the destruction of rain forests

    C. will lead to the destruction of rain forests

    D. will not destroy the rain forests

48. Bio-fuels might _____.

    A. drive food prices up

    B. drive food prices down

    C. have little or no impact on food prices

    D. cut into food prices

49. The increased production of palm oil _____.

    A. just affects the environment

    B. just affects people

    C. affects both people and the environment

D. affects neither people nor the environment

50. The author of the report says that bio-fuels _____.

    A. have no role to play in fighting global warming

    B. can be effective in fighting global warming on their own

    C. can not fight global warming

    D. should be part of a group of measures to fight global warming

Part Four Vocabulary

Many students find the experience of attending university lectures to be a confusing and frustrating experience. The lecturer speaks for one or two hours, perhaps __(51)__ the talk with slides, writing up important information on the blackboard, __(52)__ reading material and giving out __(53)__ . The new student sees the other students continuously writing on notebooks and __(54)__ what to write. Very often the student leaves the lecture __(55)__ notes which do not catch the main points and __(56)__ become hard even for the __(57)__ to understand.

Most institutions provide courses which __(58)__ new students to develop the skills they need to be __(59)__ listeners and note-takers. __(60)__ these are unavailable, there are many useful study-skills guides which __(61)__ learners to practice these skills __(62)__ . In all cases it is important to __(63)__ the problem __(64)__ actually starting your studies.

It is important to __(65)__ that most students have difficulty in acquiring the language skills __(66)__ in college study. One way of __(67)__ these difficulties is to attend the language and study-skills classes which most institutions provide throughout the __(68)__ year. Another basic __(69)__ is to find a study partner __(70)__ it is possible to identify difficulties, exchange ideas and provide support.

51. A. extending	B. illustrating	C. performing	D. conducting
52. A. attributing	B. contributing	C. distributing	D. explaining
53. A. assignments	B. information	C. content	D. definition
54. A. suspects	B. understands	C. wonders	D. convinces
55. A. without	B. with	C. on	D. except
56. A. what	B. those	C. as	D. which
57. A. teachers	B. classmates	C. partners	D. students

58. A. prevent   B. require   C. assist   D. forbid
59. A. effective   B. passive   C. relative   D. expressive
60. A. Because   B. Though   C. Whether   D. If
61. A. enable   B. stimulate   C. advocate   D. prevent
62. A. independently   B. repeatedly   C. logically   D. generally
63. A. evaluate   B. acquaint   C. tackle   D. formulate
64. A. before   B. after   C. while   D. for
65. A. predict   B. acknowledge   C. argue   D. ignore
66. A. to require   B. required   C. requiring   D. are required
67. A. preventing   B. withstanding   C. sustaining   D. overcoming
68. A. average   B. ordinary   C. normal   D. academic
69. A. statement   B. strategy   C. situation   D. suggestion
70. A. in that   B. for which   C. with whom   D. such as

Part Five   Short Answer Questions

Directions: *In this part there is a short passage with five questions or incomplete statements. Read the passage carefully. Then answer the questions or complete the statement in the fewest possible words.*

Questions 71 to 75 are based on the following passage.

A few minutes ago, walking back from lunch, I started to cross the street when I heard the sound of a coin dropping. It wasn't much but, as I turned, my eyes caught the heads of several other people turning too. A woman had dropped what appeared to be a dime.

The tinkling sound of a coin dropping on pavement is an attention-getter. It can be nothing more than a penny. Whatever the coin is, no one ignores the sound of it. It got me thinking about sounds again.

We are besieged by so many sounds that attract the most attention. People in New York City seldom turn to look when a fire engine, a police car or an ambulance comes screaming along the street.

When I'm in New York, I'm a New Yorker. I don't turn either. Like the natives, I hardly hear a siren there.

At home in my little town in Connecticut, it's different. The distant wail of a police car, an emergency vehicle or a fire siren brings me to my feet if I'm seated and brings me to the window if I'm in bed.

It's the quietest sounds that have most effect on us, not the loudest. In the middle of the night, I can hear a dripping tap a hundred yards away through three closed doors. I've been hearing little creaking noises and sounds which my imagination turns into footsteps in the middle of the night for twenty-five years in our house. How come I never hear those sounds in the daytime?

I'm quite clear in my mind what the good sounds are and what the bad sounds are.

I've turned against whistling, for instance. I used to think of it as the mark of a happy worker but lately I've been associating the whistler with a nervous person making compulsive noises.

The tapping, tapping, tapping of my typewriter as the keys hit the paper is a lovely sound to me. I often like the sound of what I write better than the looks of it.

71. What's people's response toward the sound of a coin dropping?

72. Why do people in New York hardly hear a siren?

73. How does the author relate to sounds at night?

74. Why does he dislike the whistling?

75. What kind of sound does he find pleasant?

Part Six   Translation

Directions: *Finish the sentences on Answer Sheet by translating into English.*

76. Had I _____ (手头有足够的现金), I would have bought the apartment last year.

77. If you don't like to go shopping, you _____ (不妨待在家里).

78. It's time _____ (采取措施) about the traffic problem downtown.

79. I suggested he _____ (适应新环境) as soon as possible.

80. _____ (你不可能在北京见到他), he's gone to Paris.

81. Never in my life _____ (看到鸟巢这么美妙的建筑).

82. _____ (如果天气允许的话), the soccer game will be held as scheduled.

83. The manager asked them to take a rest, _____ (可是工人们要坚持把工作做完).

84. It's easier for kids to _____ (染上坏习惯) than to get into good ones.

85. The overseas Chinese told us a lot about the hardships _____ (他所经历的) in the U. S.

Answer Sheet

Part One   Writing

Jobs for Graduates

_____

_____

_____

_____

_____

_____

_____

_____

_____

_____

_____

_____

_____

_____

_____

_____

_____

_____

_____

_____

_____

_____

_____

Part Two   Listening Comprehension

Section A

1. [A][B][C][D]   2. [A][B][C][D]   3. [A][B][C][D]   4. [A][B][C][D]

5. [A][B][C][D]   6. [A][B][C][D]   7. [A][B][C][D]   8. [A][B][C][D]

9. [A][B][C][D]   10. [A][B][C][D]

Section B

11. [A][B][C][D]   12. [A][B][C][D]   13. [A][B][C][D]   14. [A][B][C][D]

15. [A][B][C][D]   16. [A][B][C][D]   17. [A][B][C][D]   18. [A][B][C][D]

19. [A][B][C][D]   20. [A][B][C][D]

Section C

21. _____   22. _____   23. _____   24. _____

25. _____   26. _____   27. _____

28. _____   29. _____

30. _____

Part Three   Reading Comprehension

Section A   ## Section B

31. [A][B][C][D][E][F][G][H][I][J][K][L][M][N][O]   41. [A][B][C][D]

32. [A][B][C][D][E][F][G][H][I][J][K][L][M][N][O]   42. [A][B][C][D]

33. [A][B][C][D][E][F][G][H][I][J][K][L][M][N][O]   43. [A][B][C][D]

34. [A][B][C][D][E][F][G][H][I][J][K][L][M][N][O]   44. [A][B][C][D]

35. [A][B][C][D][E][F][G][H][I][J][K][L][M][N][O]   45. [A][B][C][D]

36. [A][B][C][D][E][F][G][H][I][J][K][L][M][N][O]   46. [A][B][C][D]

37. [A][B][C][D][E][F][G][H][I][J][K][L][M][N][O]   47. [A][B][C][D]

38. [A][B][C][D][E][F][G][H][I][J][K][L][M][N][O]   48. [A][B][C][D]

39. [A][B][C][D][E][F][G][H][I][J][K][L][M][N][O]   49. [A][B][C][D]

40. [A][B][C][D][E][F][G][H][I][J][K][L][M][N][O]   50. [A][B][C][D]

Part Four   Vocabulary

51. [A][B][C][D] 52. [A][B][C][D] 53. [A][B][C][D] 54. [A][B][C][D]
55. [A][B][C][D] 56. [A][B][C][D] 57. [A][B][C][D] 58. [A][B][C][D]
59. [A][B][C][D] 60. [A][B][C][D] 61. [A][B][C][D] 62. [A][B][C][D]
63. [A][B][C][D] 64. [A][B][C][D] 65. [A][B][C][D] 66. [A][B][C][D]
67. [A][B][C][D] 68. [A][B][C][D] 69. [A][B][C][D] 70. [A][B][C][D]

Part Five   Short Answer Questions

71. What's people's response toward the sound of a coin dropping?

_____

72. Why do people in New York hardly hear a siren?

_____

73. How does the author relate to sounds at night?

_____

74. Why does he dislike the whistling?

_____

75. What kind of sound does he find pleasant?

_____

Part Six   Translation

76. _____
77. _____
78. _____
79. _____
80. _____
81. _____
82. _____
83. _____
84. _____
85. _____

Key to Model Tests

Model Test 1

Part One   Writing

What Would Happen If There Were No Power

Ever since early last century, electricity has become an essential part of our modern life. The most obvious example is that electricity lamps give us light at night. Besides, electricity is needed when we watch TV or listen to the radio. Electricity is also essential for many household appliances such as air-conditioners, refrigerators and microwave stoves. In a word, there is hardly anything in our modern life that has nothing to do with electric power.

If there were no power, our world would be in a state of confusion. For one thing, machines in factories would stop running and we would have to go without many essential industrial products. For another, our life would be seriously affected. For example, all the modern communications were shut up, running water would stop, and all the banks, schools, hospitals and post offices were closed. Without power, the result would be terrible.

Therefore, people should realize the importance of electricity and do everything to guarantee a steady supply of power. On the one hand, we should cultivate a sense of saving electric power. On the other hand, more power stations should be built and other energy resources must be found so as to provide sufficient power for the increasing demand.

Part Two   Listening Comprehension

Section A

1. A 2. D 3. D 4. A 5. D 6. C 7. B 8. D 9. A 10. D

Section B

11. C 12. D 13. B 14. A 15. A 16. B 17. C 18. D 19. B 20. A

154

Section C

21. January   22. clergyman   23. completely   24. equal   25. 1955

26. ride   27. decided   28. appealed   29. effort   30. victory

31. march   32. back

33. On August 28 that year, he led a large demonstration with many Americans taking part in.

34. Many people were moved by what he said.

35. He was killed on April 4, 1968 before another demonstration.

Part Three   Reading Comprehension

Section A

36. H   37. J   38. A   39. G   40. B   41. D   42. N   43. I   44. M   45. K

Section B

46. D   47. C   48. A   49. B   50. A   51. B   52. D   53. D   54. C   55. A

Part Four   Vocabulary

56. C   57. B   58. B   59. D   60. D   61. B   62. A   63. D   64. B   65. B

66. A   67. A   68. A   69. B   70. B   71. A   72. A   73. B   74. C   75. C

Part Five   Short Answer Questions

76. Some Differences Between Men And Women

77. The thickness of men's skin.

78. women cooler

79. more difficult or not so easy

80. slower

Part Six   Translation

81. He spent a lot of time preparing for his math exam

82. but most students have hardly made a dent in the work so far

83. spoke to her politely

84. that is why mobile phones have become so common

85. Much to our relief

Model Test 2

Part One   Writing

A letter to a Schoolmate

June 12, 2008

Dear Nancy,

I'm delighted to learn that you are going to visit me during the week-long vacation. My parents will also be happy to see you again. I'm sure you will enjoy every minute here.

I know you are fond of swimming. A river lies not far away from my home. We can go swimming there. I think it would be very pleasant and refreshing to swim in such hot summer days. In every big room of my home there is an air-conditioner. We can watch TV, play CDs or read books very comfortably at home.

A mountain about two miles away from here is beautiful and it is worth touring. We can go there on foot. When we climb to the top of the mountain, we can have a wonderful bird-eye view of the whole village.

Just phone me before you set off. There is no need for you to take anything. I'll prepare everything for you.

I am looking forward to seeing you soon.

Yours,

Liu Ying

Part Two   Listening Comprehension

Section A

1. A 2. D 3. B 4. C 5. A 6. B 7. C 8. B 9. D 10. B

Section B

11. C 12. A 13. C 14. C 15. D 16. A 17. A 18. A 19. C 20. D

Section C

21. Features   22. central   23. furniture   24. convenient

25. well-planned 26. wandering   27. signs

28. (After a meal, you can inspect the goods on sale at your leisure, and you will not be forced to buy anything)

156

After a meal, you can look at the goods without having to buy them.

29. (The goods are displayed on open shelves and counters, and it is a regrettable fact that some shoplifting goes on sometimes)

The goods are accessible to customers, so sometimes are stolen

30. (you go in, pick up a basket or a cart, walk round the shop and choose what you need)

You can choose whatever you want in it

Part Three   Reading Comprehension

Section A

31. L   32. G   33. I   34. D   35. O   36. F   37. B   38. M   39. J   40. C

Section B

41. C   42. B   43. D   44. D   45. B   46. C   47. B   48. D   49. C   50. A

Part Four   Vocabulary

51. A   52. A   53. C   54. D   55. D   56. A   57. B   58. C   59. C   60. A

61. A   62. B   63. D   64. B   65. D   66. A   67. C   68. C   69. C   70. A

Part Five   Short Answer Questions

71. increased greatly   72. mental   73. pay more

74. more drugs/medicine   75. is mainly about (or)discusses

Part Six   Translation

76. nature is being ruined

77. Tom is a mature young man

78. On weekdays the whole family were busy working

79. about the country's economic future

80. But for their help

Model Test 3

Part One   Writing

Sandstorms

Nowadays, sandstorms are getting more and more serious in the northern parts of

China, which has aroused great concern (of the whole nation).

There are many factors that have led to the abnormal climate. To begin with, the encroachment of the desert in Inner Mongolia should take the main blame for the storms. Besides, the continuous high temperature and little rain in those areas should also be responsible for the frequent occurrence of sandstorms. Last but not least, human beings should bear partial responsibility for this phenomenon because it is our destruction of vegetation and protective forests that makes the north-wind kick up the loose soil so easily and result in sandstorms.

We can resort to various ways to tackle the problem. Firstly, we should heighten people's awareness of environmental protection. Secondly, we should make laws to protect our ecological environment. Finally, we should plant more grass and protective forests to restore the vegetation and prevent sandstorms.

With the joint efforts of several generations, I believe we can eventually bring sandstorms under control and restore our ecological environment.

Part Two　Listening Comprehension
Section A
1. A　2. B　3. B　4. A　5. C　6. C　7. B　8. D　9. D　10. C

Section B
11. C　12. D　13. B　14. B　15. A　16. C　17. C　18. A　19. C　20. A

Section C
21. trouble　22. twist　23. comfortable　24. worse　25. increases

26. relax　27. frequently　28. They can only make things worse

29. (They're all rich in the nutrition that helps produce in the brain a substance that helps you fall asleep) or

They can help you fall asleep

30. (Until the start of the next morning's study and work, don't bother yourself with your sleeplessness) or

Don't bother yourself before the next morning

Part Three　Reading Comprehension
Section A
31. K　32. D　33. E　34. M　35. F 36. L　37. B　38. I　39. G　40. A

Section B

41. D 42. D 43. C 44. B 45. A 46. A 47. C 48. B 49. D 50. C

Part Four   Vocabulary

51. B 52. D 53. A 54. D 55. B 56. C 57. D 58. A 59. D 60. D
61. D 62. B 63. D 64. A 65. C 66. C 67. B 68. A 69. B 70. C

Part Five   Short Answer Questions

71. passenger planes   72. easily/with easy
73. comfortably/in comfort   74. floors   75. bright

Part Six   Translation

76. many students still failed to understand
77. No matter how hard he tried
78. it seems that she were his mother
79. as far as background color is concerned
80. Take this opportunity

Model Test 4

Part One   Writing

Practice Makes Perfect

"Practice makes perfect" is an old saying. It tells us that it does not matter if we are clumsy at doing something. As long as we keep on trying and practicing, we will do a good job in the end.

The saying is especially useful in English study. If a student is poor at listening, he does not need to lose his heart. As long as he keeps on listening to English radio programme everyday, he may do well in listening one day. And, if he is not good at speaking, he should grasp every chance to open his mouth and speak English with classmates or foreigners. His oral English may be excellent one day due to his hard work.

Not only is the saying useful in English study, it is helpful in our daily life. For example, if we are not good at playing table tennis, it is unnecessary to be discouraged. If we practice every day, we may play it skillfully one day. To an extent, there is no short cut in doing everything, since the key to success lies in "practice makes perfect".

Part Two   Listening Comprehension

Section A

1. C   2. B   3. D   4. C   5. B   6. D   7. B   8. D   9. A   10. D

Section B

11. B   12. D   13. A   14. C   15. D   16. C   17. B   18. B   19. A   20. C

Section C

21. dawn   22. attempted   23. carving   24. ancient

25. represent   26. convey   27. primitive

28. (the electronic computer, has come into being and has become increasingly important in the lives of all people)

Recently computers have appeared and become more and more important.

29. (Generally speaking, the basic job of computers is the processing of information) or

A computer's job is to process information

30. (Computers can work through a series of problems and make thousands of logical decisions without ever becoming tired) or

Computers can work out many problems and make logical decisions without being tired

Part Three   Reading Comprehension

Section A

31. P   32. B   33. D   34. E   35. F   36. G   37. K   38. M   39. N   40. O

Section B

41. A   42. D   43. D   44. C   45. A   46. B   47. A   48. A   49. D   50. C

Part Four   Vocabulary

51. C   52. D   53. D   54. D   55. D   56. A   57. A   58. C   59. D   60. D

61. A   62. C   63. A   64. C   65. A   66. D   67. A   68. C   69. A   70. C

Part Five   Short Answer Questions

71. Some Differences Between Men And Women

72. breathe more deeply   73. The difference in pelvis   74. women

75. Blood manufacture, breathing, the size and arrangement of bones

Part Six

76. It reminds me of my grandmother

77. he obtained his Ph.D. degree one year ahead of schedule

78. Now that (Since) Professor Li has promised to attend the conference

79. As far as I know

80. but I can write out a cheque

Model Test 5

Part One Writing

The Way to Success

Everybody tries to succeed in his occupation, but someone finally achieves his goal while the other does not. Why? The successful one continues his cause to the end through long period of hard work, but the unsuccessful one is easily frustrated and gives up halfway.

To succeed, one needs three essentials—strong will, perseverance and diligence. A man, who owns strong will and perseverance, always has an inflexible spirit and sticks to his cause no matter how difficult it might be. In addition, diligence means steadiness in one's work and study. Mark often worked 15 hours a day. Life is short and we have too much to do. Without diligence one can achieve nothing.

I believe that success belongs to whoever can put up with long years of patient toil and constant efforts. This is the way to success.

Part Two Listening Comprehension

Section A

1. C　2. B　3. B　4. B　5. C　6. B　7. C　8. C　9. B　10. B

Section B

11. A　12. D　13. A　14. B　15. A　16. D　17. C　18. B　19. A　20. D

Section C

21. estimate　22. overweight　23. figure　　24. misleading　25. seek

26. worried　27. lack　　28. self-control　29. addition　　30. ideal

31. fashion　32. incredibly　33. Apart　　34. likely　　35. activity

36. healthier　37. guilty　　38. starving　　39. remove　　40. unhappiness

Part Three   Reading Comprehension

Section A

41. E 42. J 43. O 44. A 45. B 46. G 47. D 48. N 49. K 50. L

Section B

51. A 52. D 53. C 54. B 55. C 56. B 57. A 58. C 59. C 60. D

Part Four   Vocabulary

61. A 62. A 63. A 64. A 65. C 66. C 67. B 68. D 69. D 70. A
71. A 72. D 73. C 74. A 75. D 76. C 77. B 78. D 79. C 80. B

Part Five   Short Answer Questions

81. play with them

82. think up things to do

83. have to learn and develop their playing abilities gradually

84. lose their confidence and respectability

85. capable and interesting people

Part Six   Translation

86. Judging from his accent

87. she (should) go on a diet

88. I would have set off earlier

89. the house broken into

90. cheating on/in the exam

Model Test 6

Part One   Writing

A Letter of Application

Dear Sir or Madam:

I'm very happy to avail myself of the chance to recommend myself to you. My name is Kate. I'm studying in the English Department in Northwest Normal University, majoring in the English language and literature. I'm getting along with my studies quite

162

well, gaining three "Excellent students" awards in my major. Besides, I am an honest, industrious and outgoing person, which makes me very popular in and out of my class.

Then why do I choose to attend your college? I believe there are three main reasons for this. First, your college enjoys a very good reputation. Second, your college provides students with the first-class teaching facilities and a very good studying atmosphere, which is primarily important to the academic study. Finally, your college offers chances of all-round development to the promising students. Accordingly, I am applying for the admittance to your university.

Thank you for reading my letter. I'm looking forward to your kind and early reply.

Yours sincerely,

Kate

Part Two Listening Comprehension

Section A

1. B 2. B 3. C 4. B 5. A 6. A 7. C 8. D 9. B 10. B

Section B

11. D 12. D 13. B 14. C 15. C 16. A 17. D 18. A 19. C 20. B

Section C

21. pretty	22. terrible	23. dirt	24. railway	25. chimneys
26. fog	27. Disease	28. used	29. travel	30. own
31. overcrowding	32. modern	33. clear	34. motor	35. motorway
36. amount	37. industry	38. enemies	39. progress	40. countryside

Part Three Reading Comprehension

Section A

41. N 42. B 43. L 44. O 45. A 46. D 47. K 48. H 49. I 50. G

Section B

51. B 52. C 53. A 54. B 55. D 56. A 57. B 58. C 59. B 60. C

Part Four Vocabulary

61. C 62. A 63. D 64. A 65. A 66. C 67. A 68. C 69. B 70. A

71. C 72. A 73. A 74. A 75. C 76. B 77. D 78. C 79. A 80. B

Part Five Short Answer Questions

81. a fast route to wealth

82. A wreath of olive leaves / Olive wreath.

83. professional

84. He gave up running forever. / Giving up running forever.

85. ski equipment and fast food

Part Six Translation

86. For your elder brother's sake

87. ended up in prison

88. rather than losing her temper

89. subject to great suffering

90. make a fuss about such a small thing

Model Test 7

Part One Writing

On Students Paying Back the Loan

Nowadays, student loans provided by state owned commercial banks are available to more and more college students. The aim of the student loan policy is to achieve a "win-win" outcome for both college students and commercial banks.

However, to our disappointment, the proportion of students who have failed to re-pay the loans in time is high. But many other students who are able to repay refuse to pay back the student loans in time. The increase of default payment has caused greater costs and risks to banks.

As far as I am concerned, we students should increase our awareness of credit and try our best to repay the loans in time. If we are not able to, it is necessary to inform the bank concerned as soon as possible and apply for an extended repayment. Only in this way can everyone involved benefit from the student loans.

Part Two Listening Comprehension

Section A

1. C 2. B 3. D 4. B 5. B 6. B 7. A 8. C 9. B 10. D

Section B

11. B 12. D 13. C 14. C 15. D 16. A 17. B 18. A 19. D 20. C

Section C

21. essential   22. blessing   23. Obviously   24. latter   25. convenient

26. entertainment 27. comparatively 28. amusement 29. however   30. passive

31. informed   32. latest   33. fascination 34. dependent 35. dominate

36. arguments   37. criticized   38. undoubtedly 39. instruct   40. value

Part Three   Reading Comprehension

Section A

41. D 42. E 43. F 44. O 45. H 46. J 47. A 48. L 49. B 50. K

Section B

51. D 52. D 53. D 54. A 55. C 56. D 57. C 58. B 59. C 60. A

Part Four   Vocabulary

61. D 62. A 63. B 64. B 65. A 66. D 67. C 68. B 69. A 70. D

71. D 72. A 73. D 74. A 75. D 76. B 77. A 78. C 79. C 80. D

Part Five   Short Answer Questions

81. learning, intelligent behavior and the ability to solve any problems

82. dramatic instances of sudden forgetting

83. how the process of forgetting survived by evolutionary interpretation

84. adaptive ability would suffer

85. how adjustments are made between memory and forgetting

Part Six   Translation

86. to be turned down

87. the more ashamed I became

88. It is no use worrying excessively about a single failure

89. because of a minor injury in the traffic accident

90. have received more from the youth

Model Test 8

Part One   Writing

Lost and Found

On the morning of February 10, 2008, I found an MP3 in the Reference Room No. 1 on the 3rd floor of our university library.

The MP3 can be generally described as follows. The brand name of it is Sony and it is made in Singapore as stated in the label. It is brand new and white in color. The size of it is no larger than a cigarette lighter. What's more, there is a Hello Kitty sticker on its back. The owner of the MP3 may contact me now. My room number is 302 in Dormitory Building No. 5, and my room phone number and mobile phone number are (010) 82350000 and 13800000000 respectively. Please make an appointment in advance.

Sincerely Yours,
Zhang Li

Part Two   Listening Comprehension

Section A

1. C   2. A   3. B   4. C   5. D   6. B   7. A   8. D   9. D   10. C

Section B

11. C   12. A   13. D   14. C   15. B   16. D   17. C   18. A   19. D   20. C

Section C

21. experience   22. housing option   23. more than   24. requires
25. transportation   26. therefore   27. the rights and needs   28. certain rules
29. privacy and the ability to come and go at any time   30. as suitable as

Part Three   Reading Comprehension

Section A

31. K   32. O   33. I   34. N   35. F   36. B   37. M   38. L   39. G   40. D

Section B

41. D   42. C   43. B   44. C   45. C   46. C   47. B   48. A   49. B   50. D

166

Part Four   Vocabulary

51. B 52. C 53. A 54. A 55. D 56. B 57. A 58. D 59. B 60. A
61. A 62. C 63. D 64. B 65. C 66. C 67. D 68. A 69. C 70. B

Part Five   Short Answer Questions

71. The sort of brain he is born with and the sort of environment in which he is reared.
72. Environment.
73. 100.
74. Lack of opportunity blocks the growth of intelligence.
75. Intelligence and Environment.

Part Six   Translation

76. the pizza would be delivered in 20 minutes
77. in turn serves practice
78. because of lack of evidence
79. have the washing machine repaired tomorrow
80. is due to leave/depart at 10:00a.m.
81. but a generous loan from the bank pulled it through
82. unless it rains
83. The traffic on the bridge was held up for several hours
84. to operate on him as soon as possible
85. He took up teaching

Model Test 9

Part One   Writing

On Campus Lectures

Nowadays, more and more lectures are being provided to students on the campus. They are normally organized either by the department or by the Students' Union. Lectures on campus are usually in series and on different topics, such life, psychology, Chinese culture, music, etc.

Obviously, not only do such lectures broaden the students' horizon and cultivate their interests in different fields, but they also make the life of the students colorful and enjoyable.

As far as I am concerned, campus lectures are just complementary and subordinate to our school work in spite of their advantages. If Students spend too much time attending lectures, their regular study will be affected. Hence, Students should make use of their spare time to attend lectures in order to enrich their knowledge.

Part Two   Listening Comprehension
Section A

1. C   2. A   3. D   4. B   5. D   6. C   7. B   8. C   9. A   10. D

Section B

11. B   12. D   13. A   14. A   15. C   16. A   17. C   18. B   19. D   20. A

Section C

21. reputation   22. question   23. master   24. incident

25. confirmed   26. shock   27. training camp

28. charges of beating the boy to death   29. hit the boy with a beer bottle

30. attempted to run away from his stable

Part Three   Reading Comprehension
Section A

31. H   32. O   33. G   34. M   35. E   36. L   37. C   38. K   39. A   40. I

Section B

41. B   42. D   43. B   44. A   45. C   46. C   47. D   48. C   49. B   50. B

Part Four   Vocabulary

51. D   52. C   53. B   54. A   55. C   56. C   57. D   58. B   59. D   60. A

61. B   62. A   63. B   64. D   65. B   66. C   67. A   68. D   69. B   70. C

Part Five   Short Answer Questions

71. Probably because the number of scientists and engineers is decreasing.

72. such fields as law, medicine and business

73. Bright graduates and postgraduates.

74. Because they will spend much time and energy completing PH. D.

75. they don't think they can prevent themselves from working for industry

Part Six   Translation

76. finding fault with him
77. After settling all his accounts
78. interfere with the matter
79. made up of businessmen and public servants
80. did the young man become independent
81. Even though/if you don't like English
82. I would have bought the car
83. is quite sensitive to
84. the more confused I am
85. As is known to all

Model Test 10

Part One   Writing

Jobs for Graduates

Recently, Job hunting has been a headache for many college students. It was reported that about 1/3 of the graduates couldn't find jobs last years.

The reasons are various. On the one hand, a few years ago colleges and universities enrolled so many students that the number of graduates was greater than the need in the market. On the other, most graduates would rather stay jobless in large cities than go to the country.

I reckon this problem can only be solved by the combined efforts of both society and students. First, a market survey should be done to know its need. Second, students' attitude towards employment should be changed. They should be willing go to small cities. In a word, if we pay much attention, the situation can be improved.

Part Two   Listening Cornprehension

Section A

1. C 2. B 3. B 4. A 5. D 6. D 7. B 8. C 9. B 10. A

Section B

11. C 12. A 13. B 14. B 15. C 16. A 17. A 18. B 19. D 20. C

Section C

21. concerns 22. especially   23. plastic bottles 24. tap water

25. Ignore 26. inform   27. don't jog or join an expensive health club

28. sweat   29. to quench your thirst 30. feel healthy and energetic

Part Three   Reading Comprehension

Section A

31. H 32. F 33. J 34. M 35. D 36. B 37. N 38. L 39. E 40. K

Section B

41. C 42. B 43. B 44. D 45. B 46. B 47. C 48. A 49. C 50. D

Part Four   Vocabulary

51. B 52. C 53. A 54. C 55. B 56. D 57. D 58. C 59. A 60. D

61. A 62. A 63. C 64. A 65. B 66. B 67. D 68. D 69. B 70. C

Part Five   Short Answer Questions

71. They pay their attention to it.

72. Because they are besieged by so many sounds.

73. He exaggerates quiet sounds.

74. Because it reminds him of tense people.

75. The tapping of his typewriter.

Part Six   Translation

76. had enough cash on hand   77. may as well stay at home

78. to take some measures   79. should adapt himself to new environment

80. You can't have seen him in Beijing

81. have I seen such wonderful buildings as "Bird's Nest"

82. Weather permitting

83. but the workers insisted on finishing the work

84. fall into bad habits

85. he had gone through

170

Scripts for Listening

Model Test 1

Part Two   Listening Comprehension

Section A

1. **W:** Excuse me, when will the plane from New York arrive?

   M: Well, it's scheduled to arrive at 8:50 but it will be delayed more than one hour because of heavy fog at the New York airport.

   Q: What conclusion can we draw from the conversation?

2. **M:** Would you like to go to the cinema with us on Friday evening?

   W: I'd enjoy that very much if I didn't hve to take an exam next Monday.

   Q: What do you know about the woman?

3. **W:** I wonder what's happened to John? He has not been around for at least two weeks.

   M: He took a leave to see his mother in Europe.

   Q: Why is John away?

4. **M:** How many people speak English as their native tongue?

   W: Roughly imagine about two hundred and fifty million in the United States and two hundred million in the British commonwealth.

   Q: How many people are believed to be native speakers of English?

5. **W:** Look at that big field of wheat. And there's a farm with some beautiful houses.

   M: You really get to know the country when you go by train, don't you?

   Q: Where did the conversation most probably take place?

6. **M:** Let's see if the basketball game has started yet?

   W: Started? It must be clear who is winning by now?

   Q: What does the woman mean?

7. **W:** How often did you write home?

   M: I used to write home once a week.

Q: What do you understand from the man's answer?

8. **M:** Could you give me a ride to the Museum of Modern Art on your way to school?

    W: I'm sorry, but I'm not going to school today. You might ask Mary. She is leaving around half past eight.

    Q: What does the woman mean?

9. **W:** Will Jim be able to come to the meeting?

    M: I don't know yet. When I phoned just now, his friend said he had taken his girlfriend out to the movies.

    Q: What can we learn from the conversation?

10. **M:** Would you like to come with me to the theater?

    W: No, not today. I have to prepare for my class presentation now, but you can get some tickets for next Saturday.

    Q: What does the woman want to do next weekend?

Section B

Passage 1

Cambridge is about 90 kilometres northeast of London. It is one of the most beautiful places in Britain. Everything about the city of Cambridge reminds you of its famous university: students on bicycles, the atmosphere of learning, traditions and the magnificent buildings of the 30 colleges that are in the University of Cambridge. Most of the colleges stand on the bank of the Cam River a gentle river that flows through the heart of the city. Tourists and students like boating in a kind of flat bottom boat to see the colleges or to relax themselves. If the water traffic reminds the visitor of Venice, the road traffic is more likely to recall Beijing or Amsterdam. The streets are full of bicycles, hundreds and hundreds of them, they provide a cheap form of transport for the students and very conveniently of getting around Cambridge's narrow streets.

Questions 11 to 13 are based on the passage you have just heard.

11. What do tourists enjoy doing in Cambridge for relaxation?

12. Why did the road traffic in Cambridge remind one of Beijing?

13. What is the speaker's impression on Cambridge?

Passage 2

When they finished asking, Mr. Symonds leaned back in his chair and looked at each of his colleagues in turn. They nodded to him, and he said: "Well, now, my colleagues and I are completely satisfied with your replies and we feel sure that, in terms of qualifications, ability and experience, you are well suited for the post we have in mind. But we are faced with a certain difficulty. If we employ you, it means we must place you in a position of authority over a number of our English employees. Many of them have been with us for a long time, and we feel sure that your appointment would upset good relations within the firm. We could not offer you the post without the responsibility, and we would not ask you to accept one or two other vacancies of a different type. These exist, but they are not suitable for someone like you, with a high standard of education and ability. So, I'm afraid, we will not be able to offer you the job."

I suddenly felt weak, and I was quite unable to think. Yet somehow I managed to leave that office, go along the corridor and down the lift, and walk out into the busy sunlit street.

I had just been brought face to face with something that I had either forgotten or completely ignored since the six exciting years of the war—my own black skin.

Questions 14 to 16 are based on the passage you have just heard.

14. According to Mr. Symonds, why couldn't they offer him a job?

15. What is the real reason that they didn't want to offer a job?

16. What did he respond to the refusal?

Passage 3

A young man who refused to give his name dived into the river yesterday morning to save a 12-year-old boy.

The boy, who ran away after being rescued, had been swimming in the river and had caught his foot between two concrete posts under the bridge. He shouted out for help.

At the time, a young man was riding across the bridge on his bicycle. He quickly dismounted and dived fully clothed into the river. He then freed the boy's foot and helped him to the river bank where a small crowd had collected. The boy thanked his rescuer courteously and sincerely, and then ran off down the road. He was last seen climbing over a gate before disappearing over the top of the hill.

The young man, who was about 20 years of age, said "I don't blame the boy for not giving his name. Why should he? If he wants to swim in the river, that's his business. And if I wanted to help him, that's mine. You can't have my name either!"

He then ran back to the bridge, mounted his bicycle and rode away.

Question 17 to 20 are based on the passage you just heard.

17. How old is the boy?

18. What happened yesterday morning?

19. What did the boy do after being rescued?

20. According to the passage, which statement is not true?

Section C

A passage with 15 missing words

Martin Luther King, Jr. was born in Atlanta, Georgia, on (21) January 15, 1929. He was a black (22) clergyman, who devoted himself (23) completely to the struggle for (24) equal rights for the black people and an end to segregation in the South of the United States. In (25) 1955, he organized a black boycott of the city buses in Montgomery, Alabama. The black people there had (26) decided that they would no longer (27) ride in segregated buses. Led by King, they (28) appealed to the courts for support of their (29) effort. The boycott against segregation lasted 381 days, and ended in (30) victory the next year.

In the spring of 1963, he began to organize a (31) march to Washington to persuade the U. S. government to (32) back a mass Civil Rights Movement for black people. (33) On August 28 that year, he led a large demonstration with many Americans taking part in. From all over the country, citizens came to "march on Washington" in support of civil rights legislation. It was then that King delivered the most impressive speech of his career. (34) Many people were moved by what he said.

In 1964, at the age of only 35, he was awarded the Nobel Peace Prize. (35) He was killed on April 4, 1968 before another demonstration.

Model Test 2

Part Two　Listening Comprehension

Section A

1. **M:** Good morning! This is David speaking. I'm just ringing to confirm my appointment with Dr. Li for this afternoon.

   W: Yes, Dr Li's expecting you at 2 o'clock.

   Q: Why is the man making the phone call?

2. **W:** How long will it take you to fix my computer?

   M: I'll call you when it's ready, but it shouldn't take longer than a week.

   Q: What's the probable relationship between the speakers?

3. **M:** Have you a table for four?

   W: Certainly, sir. A corner table or would you rather be near the window?

   Q: What is the man doing?

4. **W:** I need some new clothes. None of my trousers fits.

   M: Maybe you should go on a diet.

   Q: What does the man mean?

5. **M:** Linda is doing a part-time job next week.

   W: Shouldn't she concentrate on her homework instead?

   Q: What does the woman suggest?

6. **W:** Do we have enough time for the 7:30 train if we get out right away?

   M: No, it's too late. It's impossible for us to get to the station in 20 minutes.

   Q: What time is it now?

7. **M:** I've got to go now. I have to catch the last train.

   W: But it's too late. You should have said so earlier.

   Q: What does the woman mean?

8. **W:** Have you read the latest novel "Henry Porter"?

   M: I've just finished it. I really recommend it.

   Q: What are the man and woman talking about?

9. **M:** I'd like to return these books.

   W: Let me see. These books are one week overdue. I'm sorry, but you'll have to pay a fine.

   Q: What does the woman mean?

10. **W:** Did you watch the basketball match last night?

    M: Oh, yes. It was supposed to start at 7:30. but it was delayed 15 minutes.

    Q: When did the basketball match start?

Section B

Passage 1

A six-year-old boy has been found alive after spending four days and five nights in an icebox that was buried under tons of ruins in Thursday's big earthquake.

The boy, Tom, was found early yesterday in the village of Sem as rescuers were working to pull his father out of the ruins of their home.

Hearing a faint cry of "Get me out, get me out", rescuers dug down another 1.5m and found the boy in the icebox. He was pronounced in a good condition, suffering only four or five slight wounds.

Tom's eight brothers and sisters died in the earthquake, which officials say may have killed as many as 50,000 people.

By Sunday foreign doctors were leaving the earthquake areas as hope had faded of finding any more survivors.

Questions 11 to 13 are based on the passage you have just heard.

11. What happened to the boy in the earthquake?

12. How many days had passed before the boy was rescued?

13. How did the boy survive the big earthquake?

Passage 2

Ralph guided the car slowly, very slowly down the road toward the hospital. Fortunately there were no other cars on the hill as he went down the slippery road. Ralph could not hear Mrs. Smith breathing. Was she already dead? He must get her to the hospital! Only three more blocks. Ralph had just crossed the intersection when he saw the flashing red light of a police car behind him. There were two policemen in the car; the one on the near side rolled down his window and shouted for Ralph to pull over. "Is this your car, Kid? Your license plates are a little out of date, you know. Let me see your driver's license." "But we can't stop now," said Ralph. "The woman in the back seat is really sick. This is an emergency!" The policeman was surprised. "Under normal circumstances, you'd be in big trouble. But I agree you had no choice. Put the woman in our car. We'll take her to the hospital." The police car zoomed away, leaving Ralph sitting in the front seat of his car.

Questions 14 to 16 are based on the passage you have just heard.

14. What was Ralph trying to do?

15. Why did the police stop him?

16. What did the police decide to do to Ralph?

Passage 3

Susan Anthony was born in Massachusetts in 1820 and died in Rochester, N.Y., in

1906. In the 1850s, she saw many problems in her country and wanted to do something about them.

One of these problems was that women did not have the right to vote in the United States. Susan Anthony and many others felt that women and men should have equal rights. In 1860 she helped start the National Women's Association. This group worked hard to get women the right to vote in the United States.

In 1869, the state of Wyoming gave women the right to vote. Some other states also allowed women to vote. But Susan Anthony and the National American Women's Association wanted all women to have the right to vote. They worked to add this to the Constitution of the United States. Finally, in 1920, fourteen years after Susan Anthony's death, an article was added to the Constitution. It gave all American women the right to vote.

Question 17 to 20 are based on the passage you just heard.

17. What did Susan Anthony think about her country?

18. Who among the American women had the right to vote before 1920?

19. When did all women finally get the right to vote in the United States?

20. What do we learn about Susan Anthony form the passage?

Section C

A passage with 10 missing words

One of the (21) <u>Features</u> of large modern cities is the number of big department stores, most of which are to be found in or near the (22) <u>central</u> area. They're vast buildings many stories high, where you can buy almost anything you need, from a box of toothpicks to a suite of (23) <u>furniture</u>. Most of them are very modern and are equipped with (24) <u>convenient</u> elevators and escalators, and have (25) <u>well-planned</u> lighting, air-conditioning and ventilation. You can spend hours (26) <u>wandering</u> around in one of these department stores, and you will probably lose your way while you are doing so, in spite of the many (27) <u>signs</u> pointing the way to the elevators and exits.

If you have been in one of these stores so long that you feel hungry, you and your family will not need to leave the building, for nearly all the big stores have cafes, snack bars or restaurants in them. (28) <u>(After a meal, you can inspect the goods on sale at your leisure, and you will not be forced to buy anything)</u> or <u>After a meal, you can look at the goods without having to buy them</u>, though occasionally an assistant may ask you whether he or she can be of help to you.

Another feature of Shanghai's shopping life is the chain-store, in which prices are lower than in the big store, and a wide variety of goods are offered—chiefly foodstuffs, household goods, clothing and stationery. (29) (The goods are displayed on open shelves and counters, and it is a regrettable fact that some shoplifting goes on sometimes.) or The goods are accessible to customers, so sometimes are stolen, in spite of the vigilance of the store security guards.

A lot of the food stores in Shanghai now operate on the "serve yourself" system: (30) (you go in, pick up a basket or a cart, walk round the shop and choose what you need) or You can choose whatever you want in it. At the exit there are a number of counters where you pay for all your purchases together.

Model Test 3

Part Two   Listening Comprehension

Section A

1. **W:** Believe it or not, Tom has come out of the traffic accident.

   M: That's true. But his car is a total wreck, you know.

   Q: What do you learn form the conversation?

2. **M:** The show on the Ancient costume was very interesting.

   W: Very interesting? I could spend hours there.

   Q: What did you know about the woman?

3. **W:** Here's a 10-dollar bill, give me two tickets for tonight's show please.

   M: Sure. Two tickets and here's $1.40 change.

   Q: How much does one ticket cost?

4. **M:** What happened to you? You are so late.

   W: The bus I took broke down in front of the hospital and I had to walk form there.

   Q: Why was the woman so late?

5. **W:** I went to a concert last night. They played beautifully. Do you like symphony?

   M: I like symphony, but not as much as folk music.

   Q: What did the man say about symphony?

6. **M:** How does your son like his new job?

   W: Fine. He seems to have made new friends in no time.

Q: What can be inferred about the woman's son?

7. **W**: What shall we do on Saturday, go sightseeing, go camping or stay home?

   M: I don't think I can deal with the crowds and the traffic. Let's stay here and relax.

   Q: Why isn't the man willing to go out?

8. **M**: Judy, have you met Jack recently?

   W: Oh, yes. To my surprise, he's no longer the man he was two years ago.

   Q: What does the woman mean?

9. **W**: I heard your brother has been to an interview today. How did it go?

   M: Oh, if he had just relaxed, he would have done fine.

   Q: What can we learn about the man's brother?

10. **M**: Let's see if the basketball game has started yet?

    W: started? It must be clear who is winning by now?

    Q: what does the woman mean?

Section B

Passage 1

This library is an English language teaching and learning library. Unfortunately our resources are limited and so not everybody can join. Teachers of English, university students, and professionals who are in the medical, engineering, and management fields can all join the library. Those from other professions are welcome to apply, but your application will not necessarily be approved.

You must fill in a library application form and put it in the box on the librarian's desk. Because of the high number of applications we receive each week, you must wait one week. Please bring your student or work card to pick up your library cards. Library application forms which are not picked up within 2 months will be discarded and you will have to reapply.

You may borrow one video at a time. The video must be returned in one week. If you cannot return it on time, please call, otherwise your video library card will be canceled. You may borrow 3 items at one time, that is 3 books or 3 cassettes. Items must be returned within one month. You can telephone the library to renew items for another month.

Questions 11 to 13 are based on the passage you have just heard.

11. Why can't the library issue library cards to everyone who applies?

12. What will the library do if a reader fails to renew the video when it is due?

13. For how long can a reader keep the book before he renews it?

Passage 2

Around the year 1000 A.D. some people from northwest India began to travel west-ward. Nobody knows why. After leaving their homes, they did not settle down again, but spent their lives moving from one place to another, their later generations are called Romany people, or Gypsies. There're Gypsies all over the world, and many of them are still travelling with no fixed homes. There are about 8,000,000 of them, including 3,000,000 in eastern Europe. Gypsies sometimes have a hard time in the countries where they travel, because they are different, people may be afraid of them, look down on them, or think they are criminals. The Nazis treated the Gypsies cruelly, like the Jews, and nobody knows how many of them died in Hitler's death camps. Gypsies have their own language Romany. They like music and dancing. And they often work in fairs and travelling shows. Travelling is very important to them, and many Gypsies are unhappy if they have to stay in one place. Because of this, it is difficult for children to go to school, and Gypsies are often unable to read and write. In some places, the education authorities tried to arrange special travelling schools for Gypsy children so that they can get the same education as other children.

Questions 14 to 16 are based on the passage you have just heard.

14. Why did the ancestors of Gypsies leave their home?

15. What is the attitude of some people toward Gypsies?

16. What measure has been taken to help Gypsy children?

Passage 3

There's a marked tendency for most developed countries to grow steadily noisier each year. This continually increasing amount of noise is uncomfortable and, what is more im-portant, can affect our health. The noise of machines, heavy traffic and airplanes consti-tutes perhaps the most serious threat to public health. Such noise can interfere with our ability to converse, it can disturb our sleep, and it can quickly make us become nervous wrecks. A loud blast or an explosion may even cause damage to our hearing. But there's another danger-just as great. This is the gradual damage which may be caused if we're continually exposed to noise over several years. Fortunately, technology is progressing at a very rapid rate. Some manufacturers are now designing new silencing mechanisms in their products, and planning experts are even beginning to plan cities according to sound zones.

Questions 17 to 20 are based on the passage you have just heard.

17. According to the passage, which statement is true?

18. What is not mentioned about noise-making in this passage?

19. What harm does noise make to our health?

20. How do people try to solve the problem?

Section C

A passage with 10 missing words

Do you have (21) <u>trouble</u> sleeping at night? Then, maybe, this is for you:

When you worry about not being able to sleep and (22) <u>twist</u> around, trying to find a (23) <u>comfortable</u> position, you're probably only making matters (24) <u>worse</u>. What happens is that your heart rate actually (25) <u>increases</u>, making it more difficult to (26) <u>relax</u>. You may also have some bad habits that contribute to the problem. Do you rest (27) <u>frequently</u> during the day? Do you get almost no exercise or do you exercise strenuously late in the day? Do you think about sleep a lot or sleep late on the weekend?

Any or all these factors might be leading to your insomnia by disrupting your body's natural rhythm. What should you do then on those sleepless nights? Don't bother with sleeping pills. (28) <u>They can only make things worse</u>. The best thing to do is to drink some milk or eat some cheese or tuna fish. (29) <u>(They're all rich in the nutrition that helps produce in the brain a substance that helps you fall asleep)</u> or <u>They can help you fall asleep</u>. This will enable you to relax and you'll be on the way to get a good night's sleep. (30) <u>(Until the start of the next morning's study and work, don't bother yourself with your sleeplessness)</u> or <u>Don't bother yourself before the next morning</u>. Think about this: when the morning comes, everything will be all right again.

Model Test 4

Part Two   Listening Comprehension

Section A

1. **M:** Have you found anything wrong with my heart?

W: Not yet. I'm still examining. I'll tell you the result next Tuesday.

Q: What's the probable relationship between the man and the woman?

2. **W:** Would you please close the window? I feel a bit cold.

   M: Oh, I'm sorry, but maybe you should put on your sweater. We need some fresh air.

   Q: What does the man think the woman should do?

3. **M:** Excuse me, I've a ticket for the 6 o'clock flight to New York. But I'm afraid I can't make it. Is there a seat available for tomorrow morning?

   W: Let me see. I'm sorry. All the morning flights have been booked up. The earliest we can get for you is the 2 o'clock flight in the afternoon.

   Q: What does the conversation tell us?

4. **W:** I think we'd better paint our house pink.

   M: Why not white?

   Q: What does the woman mean?

5. **M:** good afternoon, madam. Would you like to sit here? I'm afraid there are no other seats free at the moment.

   W: I'd prefer to sit alone but I suppose this will do. Have you a menu, please?

   Q: What is the probable relationship between the man and the woman?

6. **W:** How long does it take you to ride home when there is not much traffic?

   M: Only twenty-five minutes. But if I can't leave my office before 5:30 p.m., it sometimes takes me 35 minutes.

   Q: How long does it take the man to ride home when it isn't in rush hour?

7. **M:** Congratulations. I understand you've got a job. When will you start to work?

   W: You must be thinking of someone else, I'm still waiting to hear the good news.

   Q: What does the woman mean?

8. **W:** We'd better hurry, Eugene. There is not much time left. The train is to leave at 10 o'clock.

   M: Don't worry. We still have half an hour.

   Q: What time was it when the conversation took place?

9. **M:** Professor Liu, we were wondering if we could sit in on your English class?

   W: I wish I could say yes, but if I accepted you two, I wouldn't know how to say no to a lot of others who have the same request.

   Q: What does the woman mean?

182

10. **W**: Would you mind helping me with this luggage?

   M: Of course not.

   Q: What does the man mean?

Section B

Passage 1

Tom had worked 30 years for the same company and now he had to retire. As a sign of gratitude, the company held a dinner in his honor. "Tom" announced his boss, "It's my great honour to present this gift to you on behalf of the company." Tom walked down to the front of the table and accepted the gift with pride. It was a gold watch and on it was written "To faithful Tom for 30 years of service." Tom wept. "I am at a loss for words." At home, Tom's wife looked at the gold watch critically. "For this you worked 30 years? A cheap gold-plated watch?" "It's the thought dear." answered Tom. "The important thing is that I am not working any more." His wife held the gold watch to her ear and said: "Neither is your watch."

Questions 11 to 13 are based on the passage you have just heard.

11. What did the company do to honor Tom?

12. How did Tom feel when he saw what was written on the watch?

13. What can we infer from the story?

Passage 2

I flew to San Francisco to take care of some business with Mr. Jordan. But as soon as I arrived, I got sick and couldn't meet with him. I had to call our appointment off. Then, when I felt better I thought about visiting him at his home, but he lived too far away. I tried to telephone him during office hours, but he was busy. The receptionist said that Mr. Jordan would call me back, but he didn't. I gave up trying to make a new appointment because it would take more time and effort and I called out to him. It was someone else. When I returned to my hotel that day, I found a message, which said that Mr. Jordan had gone out of town on some sudden unexpected business. I was sorry I had missed seeing him, but I really enjoyed my sightseeing in San Francisco.

Questions 14 to 16 are based on the passage you have just heard.

14. Why couldn't the speaker meet Mr. Jordan when he got to San Francisco?

15. Why did the speaker give up making another appointment?

16. What do we learn form the story?

Passage 3

Mike Wilson worked as a low rank official in the War Office during the early 1940s. Though he didn't hold an important position, he got along very well with almost everybody, and was believed in by most of his leaders.

One day, Wilson arrived at his office in an expensive car. Little as his pay was, he appeared to have got a lot of money to spend. He bought an expensive house and gave one party after another. At one of the parties he met a beautiful woman and fell in love with her. When he was asked by the woman one evening how he had suddenly go so much money to spend. Wilson explained that he had a very rich uncle who lived abroad and posted him money nearly every month. But his story could not fool the woman. She was a policewoman and was sent to watch him closely by acting as his "girlfriend", because the police had noticed that he often stayed behind in the evenings and was usually the last person to leave the War Office.

His "girlfriend" and three other policemen entered his house when he was out and discovered copies of government secret papers and radio transmitter hidden inside a piano. After Wilson was caught, it was learned that his real name was Jack Brown, and that he had been hired as a spy for the Germans.

Question 17 to 20 are based on the passage you have just heard.

17. When did the story take place?

18. What do we learn about Wilson's "girlfriend"?

19. Why did Wilson often stay late in his office?

20. What was found out about Wilson at last?

Section C

A passage with 10 missing words

Since the (21) dawn of history, men have gathered information and have (22) attempted to pass it on to other men. The (23) carving of word-pictures on the walls of (24) ancient caves as well as hieroglyphics(象形文字) on stone tablets (25) represent some of man's earliest efforts to (26) convey information. Evidently, these efforts were very simple and (27) primitive.

But as civilizations grew more complex, better methods of communication were

184

needed. The written word, carrier pigeons, the telegraph and many other devices carried ideas faster and faster from man to man but still not fast enough to satisfy ever-growing needs. In recent years, as men entered the information epoch, a new type of machine, (28) (the electronic computer, has come into being and has become increasingly important in the lives of all people) or Recently computers have appeared and become more and more important. With the invention and development of computers, it is as if man has suddenly come upon Aladin's magic lamp.

(29) (Generally speaking, the basic job of computers is the processing of information) or A computer's job is to process information. For this reason, computers can be defined as devices which accept information, perform mathematical or logical operations with the input information, and then supply the results of these operations as new information.

(30) Computers can work through a series of problems and make thousands of logical decisions without ever becoming tired)-or Computers can work out many problems and make logical decisions without being tired. However, although computers can replace men in dull, routine tasks, they only work according to the instructions given them, in other words, they have to be programmed. Their achievements are not very spectacular when compared to what the minds of men can do.

Model Test 5

Part Two   Listening Comprehension

Section A

1. **M:** Are you ready to check out?

   W: Yes. You pay the bill and I'll call the desk and have our luggage taken out to the taxi.

   Q: Where does this conversation most probably take place?

2. **W:** How Tom ever got the job with so many others applying? I just don't understand it.

   M: It must have been the beginner's luck.

   Q: Why is the woman puzzled?

3. **M:** I hear you have an apartment for rent. Can I take a look at it?

   W: Sure, you're welcome anytime for appointment. But I have to tell you the building is close to a railway and if you can't put up with the noise you might as well save yourself a trip.

   Q: What do we learn from the conversation?

4. **M:** How's John now? Is he feeling any better?

   W: Not yet. It still seems impossible to make him smile. Talking to him is really difficult, and he gets upset easily over little things.

   Q: What do we learn about John from the conversation?

5. **M:** I think it's starting to snow.

   W: Starting to snow? Look, the grounds are already white.

   Q: What does the woman mean?

6. **M:** Good afternoon, madam. Would you like to sit here? I'm afraid there are no other seats free at the moment.

   W: I'd prefer to sit alone but I suppose this will do. Have you a menu, please?

   Q: What is the probable relationship between the man and the woman?

7. **M:** How many rooms do you want in a house?

   W: Well, to begin with, one bedroom for each of the children and one for us. And I want a bathroom, a big kitchen and a living room with lots of sunlight in it. Yes, altogether seven rooms.

   Q: How many children do they have?

8. **W:** Here's an ad for an apartment with two bedrooms. It's near the campus and not too small.

   M: What's the number? I'll find out if it's available for immediate occupancy.

   Q: What are the man and woman doing?

9. **W:** You must have enjoyed using your new camera on your trip.

   M: I would have, but after buying a new camera especially for that trip, I left it in the car with my friend who drove me to the airport.

   Q: What do we learn from the conversation?

10. **W:** There is a new chef at the restaurant in the shopping mall.

    M: It remains to be seen whether the new one is any better than the old one.

    Q: What does the man mean?

Section B

Passage 1

When I first went to London as a student, I sat alone during parties with my glass of wine. I hoped people would think that I was having great thoughts and that someone might come up to me and say "Excuse me, I hope you won't mind my coming up to you

186

like this. I don't want to interrupt your thoughts. But really, you are the only interesting-looking person in the room. May I talk to you?" It never happened. Here is some advice if you would like to be a good conversationalist. Be an attentive listener. Encourage others to talk about themselves. To be interesting, be interested. Ask questions that other people will enjoy answering. Encourage them to talk about themselves and what they have done. Remember that the people you are talking to are a hundred times more interested in themselves and their problems than they are in you and your problems. A person's toothache means more to that person than a famine in Africa which kills a million people. A pain in one's arm interests one more than forty earthquakes in America. Think of that the next time you start a conversation. Diogenes, the Greek philosopher who is supposed to have lived in a barrel, said, "The reason why we have two ears and only one mouth is so that we may listen more and talk less."

Questions 11 to 13 are based on the passage you have just heard.

11. What happened to the speaker at parties?

12. Why should we encourage others to talk about themselves in order to be good conversationalists?

13. What can we learn from what the Greek philosopher said?

Passage 2

Several days ago three lions escaped from a circus due to the carelessness of one of the keepers. Two of the lions headed for the grassland not far away, where they were immediately caught by their trainer. The third one, however, went into town and when he saw an open window on the first floor of a private home, he jumped in. Inside, he found an elderly lady whose eyesight was failing. She thought the animal was a large dog and patted it on the head. The wild beast paid no attention to her and went into the bedroom, where it fell fast asleep on the carpet. It was there that the trainer found the lion. He and his helpers put him in a cage and carried him back quietly to the circus.

Questions 14 to 16 are based on the passage you have just heard.

14. How did the lion escape?

15. Where did two of the lions go?

16. Why wasn't the old man afraid?

Passage 3

What does the word "library" mean to you? Do you think a library is a large, silent room containing hundreds of books? It may surprise you to learn that there are other kinds of libraries. Most libraries do lend books, but some also lend art, music, and even toys.

In some libraries, you can borrow an excellent reproduction of a famous painting for your home for several weeks. Then, you can return it and bring another one home.

This is also true for records. You may choose your favorite record and take it home. There you may listen to it as often as you like. Later you may return it and try something else.

Toy-lending is a new idea in libraries. In a toy library children's toys and games are classified by age groups just as books usually are. Children may play with anything in the library, and instead of demanding silence, toy libraries encourage children to make noise! Toy libraries not only provide toys and games for children, but also give them a place to come meet and play with other children.

Question 17 to 20 are based on the passage you have just heard.

17. What are some of the things that you can borrow from an art library?

18. What is toy-lending?

19. In what kind of library can children make as much noise as they want?

20. Apart from toys and games, what else do toy libraries provide for children?

Section C

A passage with 20 missing words

Doctors(21) estimate that about 40% of women over thirty in Britain are (22) overweight. This (23) figure may be (24) misleading as a large number of overweight people never (25) seek medical advice. Many women are very (26) worried about being overweight. They feel that it shows a (27) lack of will-power or (28) self-control on their part. In (29) addition, fat women do not conform to the modern (30) ideal of beauty exemplified by (31) fashion models and young film stars who are (32) incredibly thin. (33) Apart from aesthetic reasons, there are strong medical grounds for not overeating. Overweight people are particularly more (34) likely to get heart disease and are easily tired by physical (35) activity. Losing weight would certainly make them feel (36) healthier and increase their life expectancy.

Some women feel (37) guilty about being fat and their guilt is expressed by eating more. It is a vicious circle. On the other hand, there are women who unnecessarily lose weight in order to conform to a model of social acceptability. Some of them end up (38) starving themselves to death! So perhaps it might be better to try to (39) remove fat people's (40) unhappiness than to try to remove the fat.

Model Test 6

Part Two   Listening Comprehension

Section A

1. **W**: Mary missed her class again, didn't she?

   M: Well, she went to the 10 o'clock lecture that lasted for one hour, but she left when it was half over.

   Q: When did Mary leave?

2. **M**: Hi, Jane, sorry to take you away from the kitchen, but it seems as if something has come up. Stacey's off to New York, so do you know who might replace her?

   W: That's a tough one but I'll certainly keep an eye out for someone.

   Q: Where does the conversation most probably take place?

3. **W**: I went to a concert last night. They played beautifully. Do you like classical music?

   M: I like classical music, but not as much as jazz.

   Q: What did the man say about classical music?

4. **M**: Did you pick up your clothes from the laundry today?

   W: No, I was too busy to find time for it.

   Q: What happened to the clothes?

5. **M**: What do you think of Professor White's English class?

   W: Well, his lectures are interesting enough, but I think he could choose more appropriate questions for the tests.

   Q: What is the probable relationship between the two speakers?

6. **W**: How do I look in my new dress?

   M: It fits you like a glove and matches your eyes perfectly.

   Q: What does the man think of the woman's new dress?

7. **M**: This physics assignment was difficult. I worked all night and couldn't finish it.

   W: You worked all night? It took me only twenty minutes.

Q: Why is the woman surprised?

8. **M:** Bob is surely so swift in class.

   W: You bet. The professor never catches him of guard.

   Q: What do we learn from the conversation?

9. **M:** Let's go for a nice long walk in the country this morning.

   W: I certainly would go with you, but I think I'm under the weather.

   Q: What can we infer from the conversation?

10. **W:** I'm sorry I have caused your uncle so much trouble.

    M: Don't worry about it. He is the sort of man who is never happy unless he has something to complain about.

    Q: What can we learn about the man's uncle?

Section B

Passage 1

Throughout history, people have been interested in knowing how language first began, but no one knows exactly where and how this happened. However, we do know a lot about the languages of today and also the languages of earlier times. There are probably about 3,000 languages in the world today. Chinese is the language with the most speakers. English, Hindi, Urdu, Russian and Spanish are also spoken by millions of people. On the other hand, some languages have less than one hundred speakers.

There are several important families of languages in the world. For example, most of the languages of Europe are in one large family called Indo-European. The original language of this family was spoken about 4,500 years ago. Many of the present-day languages of Europe and India are modern forms of it.

Languages are always changing. The English of today is very different from the English of 500 years ago. In time, some even die out completely. About 1,000 years ago English was a little-known relative of German spoken on one of the borders of Europe.

Questions 11 to 13 are based on the passage you have just heard.

11. How many languages are spoken in the world today?

12. What do we learn about the Indo-European language family?

13. What is the passage mainly about?

Passage 2

Marriage is still a popular institution in the United States, but divorce is becoming almost as "popular". Nevertheless, most American people get married at the present time. Fifty percent of American marriages end in divorce. However, four out of five divorced people do not stay single. They get married a second time to new partners. Sociologists tell us that in the next century, most American people will marry three or four times in one lifetime. Alvin Toffler, an American sociologists, calls this new social form "serial marriages". In his new book Fortune Shock, Toffler gives many reasons for this change in American marriage. In modern society, people's lives don't stay the same for very long. Americans frequently change their jobs, their homes, and their circle of friends. So, the person who was a good husband and wife can feel that their lives have become very different, and they don't share the same interests any more. For this reason, Toffler says, people in the twenty-first century will not plan to marry only one person for an entire lifetime. They will plan to stay married to one person for perhaps five or ten years, and then marry another. Most Americans will expect to have a "marriage career" that includes three or four marriages.

Questions 14 to 16 are based on the passage you have just heard.

14. What does "serial marriages" mean according to the passage?

15. According to the passage, why do some American people marry more than one person in their lifetime?

16. What is true according to the passage?

Passage 3

To get a driver's license, you must take a series of tests. The first test is the vision test. This test checks your eyes to see if you have to wear glasses when you drive. The second test is a written test that checks your knowledge of highway and traffic regulations. You can prepare for this test by studying a booklet that you can get at the driver's license office. After you pass the written test, you receive an instruction permit. This permit allows you to practise driving with an experienced driver. The last test you have to take is a road test. This checks your driving ability. If you pass it, you will receive your driving license.

When you go to the driver's license office to take the road test, you must provide your own vehicle. First, the license examiner checks the mechanical condition of your car. Then, the examiner gets into the car with you and asks you to drive in regular traffic. While you are driving, the examiner tests you for such things as starting, stopping, turning, backing and parking.

Questions 17 to 20 are based on the passage you have just heard.

17. What does the second test check?

18. What does the instruction permit allow you to do?

19. According to the passage, which of the following statements is true about the road test?

20. How many tests do you have to take before you get your licence?

Section C

A passage with 20 missing words

Life was (21) <u>pretty</u> (22) <u>terrible</u> for most people in London 100 years ago. They had to put up with noise, smoke and (23) <u>dirt</u>. The noise came from the (24) <u>railway</u>, and the smoke and dirt came from the trains and the thousands of (25) <u>chimneys</u> all around them. The smoke often mixed with (26) <u>fog</u> and hung in the air for days. (27) <u>Disease</u> killed thousands of children. Families were large but often five out of seven children would die before they were five years old.

Is life really better than it was 100 years ago? It is certainly true that people live longer than they (28) <u>used</u> to, (29) <u>travel</u> faster than they could and (30) <u>own</u> more things than they did. But we still have to put up with noise, (31) <u>overcrowding</u> and bad air. They are still a basic part of (32) <u>modern</u> life.

100 years ago there was a (33) <u>clear</u> difference between town and country. But the (34) <u>motor</u> car has changed all that. One (35) <u>motorway</u> can take up a huge (36) <u>amount</u> of land. Cars are also a basic part of modern life.

But (37) <u>industry</u> and modern life do not have to be (38) <u>enemies</u> of beauty. We can have both beauty and (39) <u>progress</u>. We need clean rivers and open (40) <u>countryside</u> just as much as people did 100 years ago. But it's becoming more and more difficult to have open land, clear water and open air.

Model Test 7

Part Two   Listening Comprehension

Section A

1. **W:** The plane leaves at 6:15. Do we have time to eat first?

   M: No. We only have 40 minutes left.

192

Q: What time is it now?

2. **M:** Well, let me look at this one. Yes, I think we can get off here and see what is on.

   W: It's an air-conditioned one, let's have a good time here instead of the theatre.

   Q: Where are they probably going?

3. **W:** How many students tried out for the basketball team this year?

   M: About 40, but only half of them have real talent for the sport.

   Q: How many students are good at basketball?

4. **W:** That's a long distance call. You'll have to call Los Angeles Information.

   M: Could you please give me the area code? I don't have a directory.

   Q: What is the woman?

5. **W:** I'm interested in the advertising job that you have offered.

   M: Oh, yes. First, fill out this form, and then someone will be with you in a few minutes.

   Q: What does the man mean?

6. **W:** I wish I could, but I'm late already.

   M: What a shame!

   Q: What does the man mean?

7. **W:** What do you think fo his experiment?

   M: He has done well considering he has no experience.

   Q: Why does he think he has done well?

8. **M:** I read a poem by E. E. Cummings last night. It is very beautiful. Do you like modern poetry?

   W: I like modern poetry, but not as much as traditional poetry.

   Q: What kind of poetry does the woman like better?

9. **M:** I paid fifteen dollars for three books, I think they're too expensive.

   W: Expensive? You shouldn't have said so.

   Q: How did the woman feel about the book's price?

10. **W:** I think I ought to buy a bigger cabinet.

    M: All you really need to do is to put away the items you rarely use.

    Q: What does the man imply about the cabinet?

Section B

Passage 1

Packaging is an important form of advertising. A package can sometimes motivate someone to buy a product. For example, a small child might ask for a breakfast food that comes in a box with a picture of a TV character. The child is more interested in the picture than in breakfast food. Pictures for children to color or cut out, games printed on a package, or small gifts inside a box also motivate many chidlren to buy products—or to ask their parents for them.

Some packages suggest that a buyer will get something for nothing. Food products sold in reusable containers are examples of this. Although a similar product in a plain container might cost less, people often prefer to buy the product in a reusable glass or dish, because they believe the container is free. However, the cost of the container is added to the cost of the product.

The size of package also motivates a buyer. Maybe the package has "economy size" or "family size" printed on it. This suggests that the large size has the most products for the least money. But that is not always true. To find out a buyer has to know how the product is sold and the price of the basic unit.

The information on the package should provide some answers. But the important thing for any buyer to remember is that a package is often an advertisement. The words and pictures do not tell the whole story. Only the product inside can do that.

Questions 11 to 13 are based on the passage you have just heard.

11. Why are people likely to buy the product sold in a glass or dish?

12. What does " A buyer wil get something for nothing" refer to according to the talk?

13. What suggestion does the speaker give us?

Passage 2

Most Americans eat breakfast and lunch quickly, unless it is a business luncheon or family occasion. And the favorite fast food in the United States is the hamburger. It seems impossible, but 3,400,000,000 hamburgers are eaten a year. This is enough to make a line of hamburgers around the world four times.

The favorite place to buy a hamburger is a fast-food restaurant. In these restaurants, people stand at the counter, order their food, wait just a few minutes and carry the food to a table themselves. They can eat it in the restaurant or take the food out and eat it at home, at work, or in a park.

Fast-food restaurants are very popular because the service is fast and the food is inexpensive. For many people, this is more important than the quality of the food. These restaurants are popular because the food is always the same. People know that if they eat a certain company's restaurant in the north or south of the city, the food will be the same; if they eat it in New York or San Francisco, it will still be the same.

Questions 14 to 16 are based on the passage you have just heard.

14. Where do people usually buy hamburgers?

15. Which of the following statements is not true?

16. What makes the fast-food restaurant more popular than the ordinary restaurants?

Passage 3

I'd like to talk about two media related issues. One of the most debated media-related issues is that many Americans are disturbed by the amount of violence their children see on television. In response to citizens' complaints, the four major TV networks agreed to inform parents of violent content at the beginning of a program, and so did the cable networks. Later, the commercial and cable networks established a rating system, based on the amount of violence, sexual content, or dirty language that a program contains. A symbol indicating the show's rating appears on the television screen at the beginning of, and continuously during, the broadcast.

Another most debated media-related issue facing Americans today has little to do with technology and much more to do with the age-old concept of personal privacy: whether any area of a person's life should remain secret once he or she becomes a public figure. A leading candidate running for president withdrew from the race after the press revealed his affair with a young woman. Politicians from both parties complained. Many critics believe that this will discourage capable people from going into politics.

On the other hand, in the old days reporters virtually plotted with politicians to keep the public from knowing about personal weakness. President Franklin Roosevelt's crippled body was not talked about or photographed. Less Americans might choose Roosevelt today, because he was dishonest by shielding the facts from the public.

Questions 17 to 20 are based on the passage you have just heard.

17. What disturbs many Americans?

18. When does the symbol indicating the show's rating appear on TV?

19. What discourages people from going into politics?

20. Why would less Americans choose Roosevelt today?

Section C

A passage with 20 missing words

Television now plays such an important part in many people's lives. It is (21) <u>essen-</u>

tial for us to try to decide whether it is a (22) blessing or a curse. (23) Obviously television has both advantages and disadvantages. But do the former outweigh the (24) latter?

In the first place, television is not only a (25) convenient source of (26) entertainment but also a (27) comparatively cheap one. People can just sit comfortably at home and enjoy an endless series of programmes rather than go out in search of (28) amusement elsewhere. Some people, (29) however, maintain that this is precisely where the danger lies. The television viewer need do nothing. He is completely (30) passive and has everything presented to him without any effort on his part. Secondly, television keeps one (31) informed about current events, allows one to follow the (32) latest developments in science and politics. Yet here again there is a danger. The television screen itself has a terrible, almost physical (33) fascination for us. We get so used to looking at its movements, so (34) dependent on its pictures, that it begins to (35) dominate our lives.

There are many other (36) arguments for and against television. The poor quality of its programmes is often (37) criticized. But it is (38) undoubtedly a great comfort to many lonely elderly people. And does it corrupt or (39) instruct our children? I think we must realize that television in itself is neither good nor bad. It is the uses to which it is put that determine its (40) value to society.

Model Test 8

Part Two   Listening Comprehension

Section A

1. **M:** How do you like Professor Zhang's history class?

   W: He's got a very strong accent. I can hardly follow him.

   Q: What do we learn from the conversation?

2. **M:** It's really a pity that Mary missed the first show last night. Jackie Chen and the other stars all showed up.

   W: She called the last minute to say John was badly hurt in an accident and was taken to hospital.

   Q: Why didn't Mary go to the first show of the new movie?

3. **W:** To teach those students English, do you have to speak their language quite well?

   M: Quite the contrary. They benefit most when the class is conducted entirely in the

196

foreign language.

    Q: Which language is used in the man's classes?

4. **M:** The English Club is having a party Friday night. Can you come?

    W: I wish I could, but I work in KFC on weekends.

    Q: Why can't the woman go to the party?

5. **M:** Have some ice-cream, Jane.

    W: I'm on a diet.

    Q: What does the woman mean?

6. **W:** What does the announcement say?

    M: It says, "This is the last call for Flight 1066 to Athens." Oh, let's hurry.

    Q: Where did the conversation most probably take place?

7. **W:** How did you English test go?

    M: I couldn't feel better about it. I finished all the questions within half an hour.

    Q: What do we know about the man's English test?

8. **M:** A table for two?

    W: Yes, please. We'd like one near the window.

    Q: What is the possible relationship between the two speakers?

9. **M:** I can't get this window open. It's really stuck.

    W: Why don't you use the screw driver and see if that works?

    Q: What does the woman suggest?

10. **M:** I need to call my mother before we leave for the airport.

    W: I'm afraid there is not much time left, why don't ask the maid to phone for you.

    Q: What does the woman suggest the man do?

Section B

Passage 1

Farmers use different kinds of soil conservation methods to protect their land against damage from farming and the forces of nature. One important form of soil conservation is the use of windbreaks.

Windbreaks are barriers formed by trees and other plants with many leaves. Farmers plant them in lines around their fields.

Windbreaks stop the wind from blowing soil away. They also keep the wind from destroying or damaging crops. They are very important for growing grains, such as wheat.

There have been studies done on windbreaks. Studies in parts of West Africa, for example, found that grain harvests can be twenty percent higher in fields protected by windbreaks. This was compared to fields without such protection.

Windbreaks can help protect a farmer's land. However, windbreaks seem to work best when they allow a little wind to pass through. If the wall of trees and plants blocks the wind completely, then violent air motions will take place close to the ground. These motions cause the soil to lift up into the air where it will be blown away.

For this reason, a windbreak is best if it has only sixty to eighty percent of the trees and plants needed to make a solid line.

Windbreaks not only protect land and crops from the wind. They can also provide wood products. These include wood for fuel and longer pieces for making fences.

Questions 11 to 13 are based on the passage you have just heard.

11. What is one important form of soil conservation?

12. Which is not the function of the windbreaks?

13. When do windbreaks seem to work best?

Passage 2

More and more students want to study in "hot" majors. As a result, many students want to give up their interests and study in these areas such as foreign languages, international business and law, etc.

Fewer and fewer students choose scientific majors, such as math., physics and biology, and art majors, like history, Chinese and philosophy. Only a few students can study in these "hot" majors, because the number of these "hot" majors is limited.

If one has no interest in his work or study, how can he do well? I learned this from one of my classmates. He is from the countryside. His parents are farmers. Though he likes biology, he chose "international business". He wants to live a life which is different from that of his parents.

In the end, he found he was not interested in doing business. He found all the subjects to be tiresome. Maybe this wouldn't have happened if he had chosen his major according to his own interests.

Choosing a major in university does not decide one's whole life. Majors which are not "hot" today may become the "hot" major of tomorrow.

Choosing your major according to your own interests is the best way to succeed.

Questions 14 to 16 are based on the passage you have just heard.

14. Why do fewer and fewer students choose scientific majors?

15. Which is NOT a "hot" major among the following subjects?

16. According to the speaker, what is the best way to succeed?

Passage 3

No one knows exactly how many disabled people there are in the world, but estimates suggest the figure is over 450million. The number of disabled people in India alone is probably more than double the total population of Canada. In the United Kingdom, about one in ten people have some disability. Disability is not just something that happens to other people: as we get older, many of us will become less mobile, hard of hearing or have failing eyesight.

Disablement can take many forms and occur at any time of life. Some people are born with disabilities. Many others become disabled as they get older. There are many progressive disabling diseases. The longer time goes on, the worse they become. Some people are disabled in accidents. Many others may have a period of disability in the form of a mental illness. All are affected by people's attitude towards them.

Disabled people face many physical barriers. Next time you go shopping or to work or visit friends, imagine how you would cope if you could not get up steps, or on to buses and trains. How would you cope if you could not see where you were going or could not hear the traffic? But there are other barriers: prejudice can be even harder to break down and ignorance inevitably represents by far the greatest barrier of all. It is almost impossible for the able-bodied to fully appreciate what the severely disabled go through, so it is important to draw attention to these barriers and show that it is the individual person and their ability, not their disability, which counts.

Questions 17 to 20 are based on the passage you have just heard.

17. According to the estimation, how many disabled people are there in the world?

18. In which country do about one in ten people have some disability?

19. Which of the following is NOT the cause of disablement?

20. What is by far the greatest barrier do disabled people face?

Section C

A passage with 10 missing words

The keys to a successful homestay (21) <u>experience</u> are understanding and flexibility.

While you or your parents may have decided that a homestay is the best (22) <u>housing option</u>, a homestay is really (23) <u>more than</u> just a place to stay during your English studies. A homestay (24) <u>requires</u> that you share living space, the telephone, and (25) <u>transportation</u> with other persons; (26) <u>therefore</u>, you will have to respect (27) <u>the rights and needs</u> of others as well. There will also be (28) <u>certain rules</u> that you will have to obey. If you require considerable (29) <u>privacy and the ability to come and go at any time</u>, a homestay may not be (30) <u>as suitable as</u> living in an apartment or other kinds of housing.

Model Test 9

Part Two   Listening Comprehension

Section A

1. **M**: How about going to a football game tonight?

   W: Sure, that sounds great. What time?

   M: About 5:00. I'll pick you up.

   Q: What will the man do to that woman?

2. **M**: Why not go out for dinner together?

   W: Which restaurant?

   Q: What can we learn from this dialogue?

3. **W**: Was your proposal accepted?

   M: It was turned down last week.

   Q: What does the man mean?

4. **M**: I'd like a room for tonight.

   W: Do you have a reservation, sir?

   W: No, I don't.

   Q: Where did the conversation most probably take place?

5. **W**: Are you ready to order?

   M: I'd like steak, but no carrots, please.

   Q: What is the possible relationship between the two speakers?

6. **W**: I need some new clothes. None of my trousers fits.

   M: Maybe you should go on a diet.

   Q: What does the man mean?

7. **W**: I wonder if I could borrow your laptop.

   M: You certainly could if I had one.

   Q: What does the man mean?

8. **W**: Do you know John Smith?

   M: That name rings a bell, but I am not sure.

   Q: What do we learn from the conversation?

9. **W**: What are you doing these days?

   M: I'm brushing up on my Japanese. I'm going to Japan next month to work for my doctor degree.

   Q: What is the man doing?

10. **W**: The plane leaves at 6:35. Do we have time to have breakfast?

    M: No, we've only got 40 minutes before the departure time.

    Q: What time is it?

Section B

Passage 1

A recent survey has shown that the number of people in the United Kingdom who do not intend to get internet access has risen. These people make up 44% of UK households, or 11.2 million people in total.

The research also showed that more than 70 percent of these people said that they were not interested in getting connected to the internet. This number has risen from just over 50% in 2005, with most giving lack of computer skills as a reason for not getting internet access, though some also said it was because of the cost.

More and more people are getting broadband and high speed net is available almost everywhere in the UK, but there are still a significant number of people who refuse to take the first step.

The cost of getting online is going down and internet speeds are increasing, so many see the main challenge to be explaining the relevance of the internet to this group. This would encourage them to get connected before they are left too far behind. The gap between those who have access to and use the internet is the digital divide, and if the gap continues to widen, those without access will get left behind and miss out on many opportunities, especially in their careers.

Questions 11 to 13 are based on the passage you have just heard.

11. According to the survey, how many people in the U.K. don't intend to get internet access?

12. Why were most people not interested in getting connected to the internet?

13. What does the passage tell us about the cost of getting online?

Passage 2

Americans love pets. Many pet owners treat their pet friends as part of the family. Some creatures such as monkeys, snakes and even wolves, find a home with some Americans. More common pets include tropical fish, mice and birds. But the favorites are cats and dogs. Americans sometimes have strong feelings about whether dogs or cats make better pets.

Leading a dog's life in America isn't such a bad thing. Many grocery stores sell delicious pet foods to owners eager to please their pets. In Houston, Texas, dogs can have their dinner delivered to their homes, just like pizza. Pets can even accompany their owners on vacation. Fancy hotels are beginning to accept both man and beast.

Why do Americans treat their pets so kindly? Beneath the luxuries, there lies a basic American belief: Pets have a right to be treated well. At least 75 animal welfare organizations exist in America. These provide services for homeless and abused animals.

The average American enjoys having pets around, and for good reasons. Researchers have discovered that interacting with animals lowers a person's blood pressure. In many cases, having a pet prepares a young couple for the responsibilities of being parents. Pets even encourage social relationships. They give their owners an appearance of friendliness, and they provide a good topic of conversation.

Questions 14 to 16 are based on the passage you have just heard.

14. What are Americans' favorite pets?

15. Why do Americans treat their pets kindly?

16. Why is it good for young couple to have a pet?

Passage 3

Liverpool city council want to clear the city of fat pigeons. They say that that people are feeding the birds, which makes them fat. The pigeons get bigger because their normal diet would consist of seeds and insects, not high-fat junk food they are eating in the city centre.

The council want people to know that everyone who feeds the pigeons is responsible for the streets being so crowded with these birds. They hope to encourage the birds to move away from the city centre and into parks and open spaces.

202

Ten robotic birds have been brought into the city centre to scare the pigeons away and visitors are asked not to give the pigeons any food. The mechanical birds—known as 'robops'—will sit on the roofs of buildings. They can be moved around to different locations. They look like a peregrine falcon, which is a bird that kills pigeons. They even make noises and flap their wings to scare the pigeons. They hope that the pigeons will go away before the city becomes the European Capital of Culture in two years.

Questions 17 to 20 are based on the passage you have just heard.

17. What do people feed the pigeons with in the city center?

18. Who is responsible for the streets being so crowded with these birds?

19. What has been done to keep the pigeons away from the city center?

20. According to the passage, which city will become the European Capital of Culture in two years?

Section C

A passage with 10 missing words

The (21) <u>reputation</u> of Japan's prized sport, sumo wrestling, is in (22) <u>question</u> after three sumo wrestlers and a stable (23) <u>master</u> were arrested in February, 2008, following an alleged hazing (24) <u>incident</u>. A 17-year old wrestler died the summer before, after collapsing in his sumo stable. Policemen later (25) <u>confirmed</u> that the boy died of (26) <u>shock</u> after being badly beaten during (27) <u>training camp</u>. Stable master, Junichi Yamamoto and three sumo wrestlers are facing (28) <u>charges of beating the boy to death</u>. Police believe Yamamoto (29) <u>hit the boy with a beer bottle</u> and ordered the beating after he (30) <u>attempted to run away from his stable</u>.

Model Test 10

Part Two Listening Comprehension

Section A

1. **M:** May I write a check for this?

   W: I'm sorry, we don't take checks.

   Q: What is the possible relationship between the two speakers?

2. **W:** I really appreciate your coming to meet me.

   M: You're welcome. How was your flight?

   Q: Where did the conversation most probably take place?

3. **M:** Will you be working at KFC tomorrow night?

  W: I'm afraid so. I wish I could get out of it.

  Q: What does the woman mean?

4. **M:** Have you got a partner to work with in English?

  W: To tell you the truth, I've been tied up with my Chinese course this week.

  Q: What can be inferred about the woman?

5. **M:** I heard Mary has been to an interview today. How did it go?

  W: Oh, if she had just relaxed, she would have done fine.

  Q: What can we learn about Mary?

6. **W:** You know, the Smiths have invested all their money in stocks?

  M: They may think that's a wise move but that's the last thing I'd do.

  Q: What is the man's opinion about Smiths' investment?

7. **W:** What do you think of Professor Wilson's lecture?

  M: The topic was interesting, but the lecture was much more difficult to follow than I had expected.

  Q: How did the man like the lecture?

8. **M:** If it hadn't been snowing so hard, I might have been home by nine o'clock.

  W: It's too bad you didn't make it. David was here and she wanted to see you.

  Q: What happened to the man?

9. **W:** I'm sorry, sir. The train is behind schedule. Please take a seat, and I'll inform you as soon as we know something definite.

  M: Thank you. I'll just sit here and read some newspapers.

  Q: What can we infer from the conversation?

10. **W:** Have you called James to come and fix the computer?

  M: I tried reaching him again and again, but it seemed his phone was out of order.

  Q: Why couldn't the man get James to come?

Section B

Passage 1

We do not know when men first began to use salt, but we do know that it has been used in many different ways throughout history. Historical evidence shows, for example, that people who lived over 3,000 years ago ate salted fish. Thousands of years ago in E-gypt, salt was used to keep the dead from decaying.

Stealing salt was considered a major crime during some periods of history. In the

18th century, for instance, if a person was caught stealing salt, he could be put in jail. History records that about ten thousand people were put in jail during that century for stealing salt! About 500 years before, in the year 1553, taking more than one's share of salt was punishable as a crime. The offender's ear was cut off.

Salt was an important item on the table of a king. It was traditionally placed in front of the king when he sat down to eat. Important guests at the king's table were seated near the salt. Less important guests were given seats farther away from it.

Questions 11 to 13 are based on the passage you have just heard.

11. How was salt used in Egypt thousands of years ago?

12. Why were the ten thousand people put in jail in the 18th century?

13. Where was the salt placed when the king had his dinner?

Passage 2

Some scientists have predicted that healthy adults and children may one day take drugs to improve their intelligence and intellectual performance. A research group has suggested that such drugs might become as common as coffee or tea within the next couple of decades.

To counter this, students taking exams might have to take drugs tests like athletes. There are already drugs that are known to improve mental performance, like Ritalin, which is given to children with problems concentrating. A drug given to people with trouble sleeping also helps people remember numbers.

These drugs raise serious legal and moral questions, but people already take vitamins to help them remember things better, so it will not be a simple problem to solve. It will probably be very difficult to decide at what point a food supplement becomes an unfair drug in an examination.

Questions 14 to 16 are based on the passage you have just heard.

14. What's the purpose for healthy adults and children to take drugs one day?

15. According to the passage, what might students have to do before taking exams?

16. What do people already take to help them remember things better?

Passage 3

A British restaurant that serves bacon and egg ice cream has been voted the best place in the world to eat in Restaurant magazine's list of The World's 50 Best Restaurants. The Fat Duck restaurant, which was runner-up last year, claimed the coveted top spot. Owner and head chef Heston Blumenthal opened his restaurant ten years ago and soon developed a reputation for highly experimental and unorthodox dishes. The menu includes leather, oak and tobacco chocolates, sardine on toast sorbet, snail porridge, and mousse dipped in liquid nitrogen. He is self-taught and has pioneered the art of "molecular gastronomy"—experiments with chemistry, physics, food and flavor that result in unique and unusual taste combinations.

Nearly 600 international restaurant owners, chefs and journalists participated in the poll to rank the best restaurants worldwide. A further thirteen British restaurants made it onto the elite restaurants list, four in the top ten. This gives the home of fish and chips an unusual reputation as a cooking paradise. Britain is infamous for its tasteless and uninspiring food, which is laughed at by the more sophisticated palates of its French neighbors. However, it seems the tide is turning: France had only eight restaurants in the top fifty and London was named in March by Gourmet magazine as the Gourmet Capital of the World. Ella Johnston, editor of Restaurant magazine, said British people are now "becoming more adventurous eaters".

Questions 17 to 20 are based on the passage you have just heard.

17. Which restaurant has been voted the best place in the world to eat in Restaurant magazine?

18. Why is tobacco important in this restaurant?

19. What has Great Britain always been famous for?

20. Who is Ella Johnston?

Section C

A passage with 10 missing words

When Americans go abroad, one of their biggest (21)concerns is, "Can you drink the water?" You may find asking yourself the same question, (22) especially in a hip, urban setting where you may notice many people, young and old, drinking from large and small (23) plastic bottles. And these people will tell you, fiercely to put the fear of God in you, that "No! You cannot drink the (24) tap water in this country anymore!"

(25)Ignore these people. These are the same kind of people who will also (26) inform you that you will drop dead before 40, or worse, become ugly, fat, and stupid if you (27) don't jog or join an expensive health club where you pay to (28) sweat. Now simply turn the tap water and drink long and deep (29) to quench your thirst. Do not be surprised the next morning if you still (30) feel healthy and energetic.

206